THE TRIADS OF IRELAND

By

PREFACE

The collection of Irish Triads, which is here edited and translated for the first time, has come down to us in the following nine manuscripts, dating from the fourteenth to the nineteenth century:—

L, *i.e.* the Yellow Book of Lecan, a vellum of the end of the fourteenth century, pp. 414*b*—418*a*, a complete copy.

B, *i.e.* the Book of Ballymote, a vellum of the end of the fourteenth century, pp. 65*b*-66*b* (ends imperfectly).

M, *i.e.* the Book of Húi Maine, a vellum of the fourteenth century, fo. 190*a*[1]-fo. 191*a*[2]. A complete copy beginning: 'Ceand Erenn Ardmacha,' and ending: 'tri hurgairt bidh a caitheam díescaidheadh (*sic*) a chaitheam iarna coir a caitheam gan altughudh.' Then follow proverbial sayings from the 'colloquy of Cormac and Cairpre,' such as: 'Dedhe ara ndligh gach maith domelar ithe ⁊ altugud. Anas deach gacha fleidhe a cainaltughudh ⁊ a mochdingbail. Caidhe deach samtha. Ni*hansa.* Gal gan forran. Deasgaidh codulta frislige,' &c., ending: 'deasgaidh aineolais imreasain. Ni d'agallaim Cormaic ⁊ Cairpre coruici sin.'

Lec, *i.e.* the Book of Lecan, a vellum of the fifteenth century. The leaves on which the Triads are found are now bound up with the codex H. 2. 17 belonging to Trinity College. It is a complete copy beginning on p. 183*b*: 'Ceand *erenn* Ardmacha,' and ending on p. 184*b*: 'ceitheora aipgitri baisi baig connailbi gell imreasain.'[1] **N**, *i.e.* 23. N. 10, a paperMS. written in the year 1575,[2] pp. 98-101. A complete copy, the gap between pp. 100 and 106 being made up by pp. 7*a*-10*b* of the vellum portion of the manuscript.

[1]By an oversight I have referred to this MS. sometimes by Lec and sometimes by H. In some cases both Lec and H will be found quoted in the variants. The same MS. is always meant.

[2]As appears from the following colophon on p. 101: 'Oraoit uaim ar do lebor a hOedh in *céd*luan iar n-aurtach Johannes. Baile Tibhaird ar bla maige mo mendad scribne hi farrad Se(a)ain hi Maoilconari. Mese (Dubthach) do scrib in ball soin da derpiris ⁊ rlæ. Anno domini 1575. Guroiuh maith ag*at*.

[Pg vi]

H', *i.e.* H. 1. 15, pp. 946-957. This is a paper manuscript written by Tadhg Tiorthach O Neachtain in 1745. It is a complete copy, with copious glosses in Modern Irish, the more important of which are printed below on pp. 36-43. At the end O Neachtain has added the following:—'Trí subhailce diadha: creidhemh, dothchus agus grádh. Trí a n-aon: athair, mac, spiorad naomh, da raibh gloir, mola[dh] ⁊ umhlacht tre bith sior tug ré don bhochtan bocht so. Aniu an 15 do bhealltuine 1745. Tadhg O Nechtuin mac Seain a n-aois ceithre bliadhna déag et trí fithchit roscriob na trithibh ṡuas.'

These manuscripts have, on the whole, an identical text, though they all occasionally omit a triad or two; and the order of the single triads varies in all of them. They have all been used in constructing a critical text, the most important variants being given in the foot-notes. The order followed is in the main that of the Yellow Book of Lecan.

There are at least three other manuscripts containing copies of the Triads. One of them I discovered in the Stowe collection after the text had been printed off. It is a paper quarto now marked 23. N. 27, containing on fo. 1*a*-7*b* a copy of the Triads, followed on fo. 7*b*-19*a* by a glossed copy of the *Tecosca Cormaic*. It was written in 1714 by Domnall (or Daniel) O Duind mac Eimuinn. Its readings agree closely with those of N. In § 237, it alone, of all manuscripts, gives an intelligible reading of a corrupt passage. For *cia fochertar im-muir, cia berthair hi tech fo glass dodeime a tiprait oca mbí*,[Pg vii] it reads: *cia focearta im-muir, cia beirthear hi tech fo glass no do theine, dogeibther occan tiprait*, 'though it be thrown into the sea, though it be put into a house under lock, or into fire, it will be found at the well.' In § 121 for *cerdai* it reads *cerd*; in § 139 it has *rotioc* and *rotocht*; in § 143 for *grúss* its reading is *grís*; in

§153 it has *aibeuloit* for *eplet*; in § 217 *tar a n-éisi* for *dia n-éisi*; in § 218*lomradh*(twice) for *lobra* and *indlighidh* for *i n-indligud*; in § 219 it has the correct reading *éiric*, and for *dithechte* it reads *ditheacht*; in § 220 it reads *fri aroile* for *fria céile*; in § 223 after *ile* it adds *imchiana*; in § 224 it reads *grís brond .i. galar*; in § 229 for *meraichne* it has *mearaigheacht*; in § 235 it has *mhamus* for *mám*; in § 236*Maig Hi* for *Maig Lii*; and for *co ndeirgenai in dam de* it reads *co nderna in dam fria*.

Another copy, written in 1836 by Peter O'Longan, formerly in the possession of the Earls of Crawford, now belongs to the Rylands Library, Manchester, where it was found by Professor Strachan, who kindly copied a page or two for me. It is evidently a very corrupt copy which I have not thought worth the trouble of collating.

Lastly, there is in the Advocates' Library a copy in a vellum manuscript marked Kilbride III. It begins on fo. 9*b*[2] as follows:—'Treching breath annso. Ceann Eirind Ardmacha.' I hope to collate it before long, and give some account of it in the next number of this series.

In all these manuscripts the Triads either follow upon, or precede, or are incorporated in the collections of maxims and proverbial sayings known as *Tecosca Cormaic*,*Auraicept Morainn*, and *Senbríathra Fíthil*, the whole forming a body of early Irish gnomic literature which deserves editing in its entirety. It is clear, however, that the Triads do not originally belong to any of these texts. They had a separate origin, and form a collection by themselves. This is also shown by the fact that the Book of Leinster, the oldest manuscript containing the [Pg viii]*Tecosca Cormaic* (pp. 343*a*-345*b*), the*Senbríathra Fíthail* (pp. 345*b*-346*a*), and the *Bríathra Moraind* (pp. 346*a*-*b*), does not include them.

It is but a small portion of the large number of triads scattered throughout early Irish literature that has been brought together in our collection under the title of *Trecheng breth Féne*, i.e., literally 'a triadic arrangement of the sayings of Irishmen.' I first drew attention to the existence of Irish triads in a note on Irish proverbs in my addition of the *Battle of Ventry*, p. 85, where a few will be found quoted. A complete collection of them would fill a small volume, especially if it were to include those still current among the people of Ireland, both among Gaelic and English speakers. I must content myself here with giving a few specimens taken at random from my own collections:—

Three kinds of martyrdom that are counted as a cross to man, *i.e.* white martyrdom, green martyrdom, and red martyrdom.—The Cambray Homily (*Thesaurus Palæohibernicus*, II., p. 246).

Three enemies of the soul: the world, the devil, and an impious teacher.—Colman maccu Beognae's Alphabet of Piety (*Zeitschrift für celtische Philologie*, III., p. 452).

Three things whereby the devil shows himself in man: by his face, by his gait, by his speech.—*Ib.*, p. 453.

Three profitable labours in the day: praying, working, reading.—Regula Choluimb Cille (*Zeitschr.*, III., p. 29).

Three laymen of Ireland who became monks: Beccan son of Cula, Mochu son of Lonan, and Enda of Arann.—Notes on the Félire of Oengus (Henry Bradshaw Society, vol. xxix., p. 112).

Three chief artisans of Ireland: Tassach with Patrick, Conlaed with Brigit, and Daig with Ciaran.—*Ib.*, p. 186.

Three poets of the world: Homer of the Greeks, Vergil of the Latins, Ruman of the Gaels.—Book of Leinster, p. 354*b*.

The three worst counsels that have been acted on in Ireland through the advice of saints: the cutting short of Ciaran's[Pg ix] life, the banishment of Colum Cille, the expulsion of Mochuta from Rathen.—Notes on the Félire of Oengus, p. 204, and Tripartite Life, p. 557.[3]

[3]Where for 'wrong stories' read 'wrong counsels' (*sanasa sáeba*). This triad is thus versified in the Brussels MS. 5100:—

Teora saoba sanasa Leithe Cuind roc[h]aras-[s]a: Mochuda cona clamhra[i]d d'ionnarba a Rathain roghlain, cur Coluim Cille tar sal, timdibhe saeghail Ciaráin.

Three things there are for which the Son of living God is not grateful: haughty piety, harsh reproof, reviling a person if it is not certain.[4]

[4]LB., p. 225 marg. inf., and Brussels MS. 5100, fo. 86*a*:

Fuil trí ní (a trí Br.) doná (danach Br.) buidech mac Dé bí: crábud úallach, coisced (coiccsed Br.) serb, écnach duine mad inderb.

Three things there are for which the King of the sun is grateful: union of brethren, upright conversation, serving at the altar of God.[5]

[5]Edinburgh MS. xl, p. 28, and Brussels MS. 5100, fo. 86*a*:

Fuil tréide dianab buidech rí gréine: óenta bráthar, comrád (fodail Ed.) cert, altóir Dé do thimthirecht.

Woe to the three folk in horrid hell of great blasts: folk who practise poetry, folk who violate their orders, mercenaries.[6]

[6]LB., p. 236, marg. inf.:

Mairg na trí lucht a n-iffirn úathmar anside: óes dogní dán, óes choilles grád, óes amsaine.

Three things there are which do not behove the poor of living God: ingratitude for his life whatever it be, grumbling, and flattery.[7]

[7]LB., p. 238, marg. inf.:

Fuil trí ní ná dlegair do bocht Dé bí: dimmda da bethaid cipé, cesacht ocus aibéle.

The following modern triads I owe to a communication from Dr. P.W. Joyce, who heard them in his youth among the people of Limerick:—

Three things to be distrusted: a cow's horn, a dog's tooth, and a horse's hoof.

Three disagreeable things at home: a scolding wife, a squalling child, and a smoky chimney.

The three finest sights in the world: a field of ripe wheat, a ship in full sail, and the wife of a Mac Donnell with child.[8]

[8]This triad comes from the Glynns of Antrim, the Mac Donnells' district.[Pg x]

In our collection an arrangement of the Triads in certain groups, according to their contents, is discernible. Thus, the first sixty-one—of which, however, the opening thirty-one are no Triads at all—are all topographical; and among the rest, those dealing with legal matters stand out clearly (§§ 149-172).

When the collection was made we have no means of ascertaining, except from internal evidence, such as the age of the language, and a few allusions to events, the date of which we can approximately fix.

The language of the Triads may be described as late Old-Irish. Their verbal system indeed is on the whole that of the Continental glosses,[9] and would forbid us to put them later than the year 900. On the other hand, the following peculiarities in declension, in which all the manuscripts agree, make it impossible for us to put them much earlier than the second half of the ninth century.

[9]I may mention particularly the relative forms *téite* 167, *bíte* 127, *ata* 75, 76,224, &c., *berta* (O. Ir. *berte*) 109, 110, *fichte* (145), *coillte* (166), *téite*(167), *aragellat* (sic leg. with

N) 171; the deponent *neimthigedar* 116, &c.;*ató*, 'I am' (104), and the use of the perfective *ad-* in *conaittig* 77, 78.

The genitive singular of *i-* and *u*-stems no longer shows the ending *-o*, which has been replaced throughout by *-a*.[10] Now, in the Annals of Ulster, which are a sure guide in these matters and allow us to follow the development of the language from century to century, this genitive in *-o* is found for the last time in A.D. 816 (*rátho, Ailello*). Thence onward the ending *-a* is always found.

[10]*rátha* 56, *foglada* 92, *flatha* 151, 248, 253; *dara* 4, 34; *Ela* 31, 35, 44 (cf.*Lainne Ela*, AU. 816); *átha* 50, *betha* 82, 83, 249.

The place-name *Lusca*, 'Lusk,' is originally an *n*-stem making its genitive *Luscan*. This is the regular form in the Annals of Ulster till the year 880, from which date onward it is always *Lusca* (A.D. 916, 928, &c.). In our text (§ 46) all the manuscripts read *Lusca*.[Pg xi]

In slender *io*-stems the dative singular in Old-Irish ends in *-iu*. I find this form in the Annals of Ulster for the last time in A.D. 816 (*Gertidiu*). Thence onward it is always *-i*, as in our text (*hi Cúailgni* 43, *d'uisci* 64).

The nasal stem *léimm* makes its nom. plur. *léimmen* in Old-Irish. In § 32 we find instead (*tair-*)*leme*. So also *foimrimm* makes its nom. plural *foimrimme* in § 163.

The word *dorus* is neuter in Old-Irish, making its nom. acc. plural either *dorus* or*doirsea*. In our text (§§ 173, 174) the word is masculine, and makes its nom. plural*doruis*.

Druimm is an *i*-stem in Old-Irish, but in the later language passes into an *n*-stem. In §51 we find the nom. pl. *drommanna*.

The neuter *grád* in § 166 makes its nom. plur. *grúda* for O. Ir. *grád*.[11]

[11]The infinitive *bith* for O. Ir. *buith* (91), the dative *cinn* for O. Ir. *ciunn* (98,135), the nom. pl. *sligthi* for O. Ir. *sligid* (which I have restored in § 49), the confusion between *do* and *di* (e.g. 83), and other details are probably due to the Middle-and Modern-Irish transcribers.

On linguistic grounds, then, I should say that our collection was made some time during the second half of the ninth century. That it cannot be dated earlier is also apparent from another consideration. Professor Zimmer has taught us to search in every ancient Irish text for indications of its having been composed either before or after the Viking period. I find no words from the Norse language in the Triads, or, if there are any, they have escaped me; but there are two distinct references to the Viking age. In § 232, a Viking in his hauberk (*Gall ina lúirig*) is mentioned as one of three that are hardest to talk to; and, in § 44, Bangor in Co. Down is called unlucky or unfortunate, no doubt, as the gloss says, because of the repeated plunderings and destruction of its monastery by the Norse during the early part of the ninth century (A.D. 823, 824).[Pg xii]

In endeavouring to trace the origin of the Triad as a form of literary composition among the Irish, one must remember that it is but one of several similar enumerative sayings common in Irish literature. Thus the collection here printed contains three duads (124. 133. 134), seven tetrads (223. 230. 234. 244. 248. 251. 252), and one heptad (235). A whole Irish law-book is composed in the form of heptads;[12] while triads, tetrads, &c., occur in every part of the Laws.[13] Such schematic arrangements were of course a great aid to memory.

[12]See *Ancient Laws of Ireland*, vol, v., pp. 118-373.

[13]Thus in the first volume of the Laws we find duads on p. 228, 15; 294, 27; triads on p. 50, 9. 27; 230, 4; 264, 20; 288, 28; tetrads 40, 21; 54, 7; 64, 1; 240, 24; 256, 4, &c.; 272, 25; 274, 3, &c.; pentads 30, 21; 50, 32; 90, 29; 102, 6; hexads 68, 11; 248, 7: a heptad 134, 9; an ennead 16, 20.

If the Triad stood alone, the idea that it owes its origin to the effect of the doctrine of the Trinity upon the Celtic imagination might reasonably be entertained. The fact that this doctrine has led to many peculiar phenomena in Irish folklore, literature, and art has frequently been pointed out. Nor would I deny that the sacred character of the number three, together with the greater facility of composition, may have contributed to the popularity of the Triad, which is certainly the most common among the various numerical sayings as well as the only one that has survived to the present day.

However that may be, I believe that the model upon which the Irish triads, tetrads, pentads, &c., were formed is to be sought in those enumerative sayings—*Zahlensprüche*, as the German technical term is—of Hebrew poetry to be found in several books of the Old Testament. I am indebted to my friend the Rev. Carl Grüneisen for the following list of such sayings, which I quote in the Vulgate version.[Pg xiii]

DUADS AND TRIADS.

Ecclus. 23: 21, Duo genera abundant in peccatis, et tertium adducit iram et perditionem, &c.

Ib. 26: 25, In duobus contristatum est cor meum, et in tertio iracundia mihi advenit: 26 vir bellator deficiens per inopiam, et vir sensatus contemptus, 27 et qui transgreditur a iustitia ad peccatum, Deus paravit eum ad romphaeam.

Ib. 26: 28, Duae species difficiles et periculosae mihi apparuerunt: difficile exuitur negotians a neglegentia, et non iustificabitur caupo a peccatis labiorum.

TRIADS AND TETRADS.

Proverb. 30: 15, Tria sunt insaturabilia, et quartum quod nunquam dicit: sufficit. 16 Inferuns, et os vulvae, et terra quae non satiatur aqua; ignis vero nunquam dicit: sufficit.

Ib. 30: 18, Tria sunt difficilia mihi, et quartum penitus ignoro: 19 viam aquilae in caelo, viam colubri super petram, viam navis in medio mari, et viam viri in adolescentia.

Ib. 30: 21, Per tria movetur terra, et quartum non potest sustinere: 22 per servum cum regnaverit: per stultum cum saturatus fuerit cibo, 23 per odiosam mulierem cum in matrimonio fuerit assumpta, et per ancillam cum fuerit heres dominae suae.

Ib. 30: 29, Tria sunt quae bene gradiuntur, et quartum quod incedit feliciter: 30 leo fortissimus bestiarum, ad nullius pavebit occursum, 31 gallus succinctus lumbos, et aries, nec est rex qui resistat ei.

Ecclus. 26: 5, A tribus timuit cor meum, et in quarto facies mea metuit: 6 delaturam civitatis, et collectionem populi, 7 calumniam mendacem, super montem, omnia gravia, 8 dolor cordis et luctus mulier zelotypa.[Pg xiv]

A TETRAD.

Proverb. 30, 24: Quattuor sunt minima terrae, et ipsa sunt sapientiora sapientibus: 25 formicae, populus infirmus qui praeparat in messe cibum sibi, 26 lepusculus, plebs invalida qui collocat in petra cubile suum.

A HEXAD AND HEPTAD.

Proverb. 6. 16 Sex sunt quae odit Dominus, et septimum detestatur anima eius: 17 oculos sublimes, linguam mendacem, manus effundentes innoxium sanguinem, 18 cor machinans cogitationes pessimas, pedes veloces ad currendum in malum, 19 proferentem mendacia testem fallacem, et eum qui seminat intra fratres discordias.

AN ENNEAD.

Ecclus. 25, 9: Novem insuspicabilia cordis magnificavi, et decimum dicam in lingua hominibus, &c.

The question arises whether these biblical sayings were the direct source from which the Irish imitations are derived, or whether the Irish became acquainted with the numerical Proverb through the medium of Greek and Latin literature. As the Irish clerics ever since the days of St. Patrick were diligent students of the Bible, there would be nothing strange in the former assumption. But there exists at least one early document which renders the latter equally possible. Under the title of *Proverbia Grecorum* we possess a collection of sayings translated by some Irish scholar in Ireland from the Greek into Latin before the seventh century.[14] Among them we find three triads,[15] two pentads,[16] three heptads,[17] and two octads.[18]

[14]This is the opinion of S. Hellmann, their latest editor. See his *Sedulius Scottus*, p. 135, in Traube's *Quellen und Untersuchungen zur lateinischen Philologie des Mittelalters*, vol. i.: München, 1906.

[15]A. 39, 41. B. 5.

[16]A. 52.

[17]A. 54. B. 3, 7.

[18]B. 1, 2.

[Pg xv]

As examples I select the following two triads:—

Tres bacheriosi(?) sunt: terribilis bellator armatus promptusque ad praelium, leo de spelunca quando praedam devorat, aper ferus de silva quando furore in aliquem irruit.

Tres sunt imperfecti qui numquam ad perfectionem vitae disciplinae pervenire possunt; tunc enim a vitiis recedunt, quando mala facere non possunt. Antiquus nauta qui multis annis seductis onmibus emere et vendere poterat; senex auriga qui in curribus et in equis Deo derelicto vana cura atque conversatione meditatur atque utitur; vetula ancilla quae dominae suae subdole in omnibus rebus quae cottidiano ministerio perficiuntur male retribuit.

Triads occur sporadically in the literature of most other nations, and have occasionally been collected. But I am not aware that this kind of composition has ever attained the same popularity elsewhere as in Wales and Ireland, where the manufacture of triads seems at times almost to have become a sport.

The wittiest triads are undoubtedly those in which the third item contains an anticlimax. Two perfect examples of this kind were composed by Heine when he tells the foreigner visiting Germany that he need but know three words of the language:*Brot*, *Kuss*, *Ehre*; and in his often quoted witticism: *Der Franzose liebt die Freiheit wie seine Braut, der Engländer wie seine Frau, der Deutsche wie seine alte Grossmutter*.

K.M.

[Pg 1]

[Pg 2]

THE TRIADS OF IRELAND

TRECHENG BRETH FÉNI INSO SÍS[1]

1. Cenn Hérenn Ardmacha.

om. BMHNLec

2. Ordan Hérenn Clúain Maic Nóis.

3. Ana Hérenn Clúain Iraird.

4. Cride Hérenn Cell Dara.

5. Sruithe Hérenn Bendchor.

6. Cóemna Hérenn Lusca.

7. Áinius Hérenn Cenannus.

8. Dí ṡúil Hérenn Tamlachta ⁊ Findglais.

dá súil L Finnglaisi N Findglais Lec

9. Tech commairce Hérenn Tech Cairnig for sligid Assail.
om. L
10. Idna Hérenn Inis Cathaig.
11. Reclés Hérenn Glenn Dá Locha.
12. Féinechas Hérenn Clúain Húama.
13. Tech Foichle Hérenn Fernæ.
14. Litánacht Hérenn Less Mór.
15. Senchas Hérenn Imblech Ibair.
16. Bérla Féine Hérenn Corcach.
17. Légend Hérenn Ross Ailithre.
Ailaicre B Elichre M
18. Téite Hérenn Tír Dá Glas.
téde N teide BM
19. Anmchairde Hérenn Clúain Ferta Brénainn.
ancairde BLec Brenainde N
20. Escaine Hérenn Lothra.
hescoemna L
21. Brethemnas Hérenn Sláine.
22. Dúire chrábaid Hérenn Fobur Féichín.
dire BM Féichín *om.* BM Fabair Feithin N
23. Áibne Hérenn Ard mBreccáin.
24. Diúite Hérenn Ross Commáin.
diuidus BM diuitecht L
25. Fáilte Hérenn Ráith mBoth nó Druimm Lethan.
26. Deṡerc Hérenn Dún Dá Lethglas.
desearc L deeirc B deirc M
[Pg 3]

THE TRIADS OF IRELAND

1. The Head of Ireland—Armagh.
2. The Dignity of Ireland—Clonmacnois.
3. The Wealth of Ireland—Clonard.
4. The Heart of Ireland—Kildare.
5. The Seniority of Ireland—Bangor.
6. The Comfort[19] of Ireland—Lusk.
[19]Or, perhaps, 'good cheer.'
7. The Sport of Ireland—Kells.
8. The Two Eyes of Ireland—Tallaght and Finglas.
9. The Sanctuary of Ireland—the House of Cairnech upon the Road of Asal.[20]
[20]A road running from Tara westward into Westmeath.
10. The Purity of Ireland—Scattery Island.
11. The Abbey-church of Ireland—Glendalough.
12. The Jurisprudence of Ireland—Cloyne.
13. The House of Wages[21] of Ireland—Ferns.
[21]Or 'hire.'
14. The Singing the Litany of Ireland—Lismore.
15. The Lore of Ireland—Emly.
16. The Legal Speech of Ireland—Cork.
17. The Learning of Ireland—Roscarbery.

18. The Wantonness of Ireland—Terryglas.
19. The Spiritual Guidance of Ireland—Clonfert.
20. The Curse of Ireland—Lorrha.
21. The Judgment of Ireland—Slane.
22. The Severity of Piety of Ireland—Fore.
23. The Delight of Ireland—Ardbrackan.
24. The Simplicity[22] of Ireland—Roscommon.
[22]Or 'uprightness.'
25. The Welcome of Ireland—Raphoe or Drumlane.
26. The Charity of Ireland—Downpatrick.

[Pg 4]
27. Trichtach Hérenn Dairchaill.
om. BM techtach E Durcaill N Darachill L
28. Fossugud Hérenn Mag mBile.
Mag Mile L
29. Martra Hérenn Tulen.
om. L
30. Ailbéimm Hérenn Cell Rúaid.
aulbeimnech L Ruadh N Ruadain L
31. Genas Hérenn Lann Ela.
32. Trí tairleme Érenn: Daire Calgaig ⁊ Tech Munna ⁊ Cell Maignenn.
om. HBM
33. Tri aithechpuirt Hérenn: Clúain Iraird, Glenn Dá Locha, Lugbad.
aithich Lec heathachbuirg M Lugmag NBM
34. Trí clochraid Hérenn: Ard Macha, Clúain Maic Nóis, Cell Dara.
clothraige BM clot*hr*ai N clochraid L clochraidi Lec
35. Trí háenaig Hérenn: áenach Tailten, áenach Crúachan, áenach Colmáin Ela.
haenaigi L Colman MSS
36. Trí dúine Hérenn: Dún Sobairche, Dún Cermna, Cathair Chonrúi.
duin NBM
37. Trí slébe Hérenn: Slíab Cúa, Slíab Mis, Slíab Cúalann.
sleibte BM
38. Trí haird Hérenn: Crúachán Aigli, Ae Chúalann, Benn mBoirchi.
hard N cích Cualann L benna LN
39. Trí locha Hérenn: Loch nEchach, Loch Rí, Loch nErni.
Rib BM Rig N
40. Trí srotha Hérenn: Sinann, Bóand, Banda.
41. Trí machairc Hérenn: Mag Midi, Mag Line, Mag Lifi.
maige HBM
42. Trí dorcha Hérenn: úam Chnogba, úam Slángæ, dercc Ferna.

doirchi L uaim Chruachan NL uaim Condba B uaim Cnodba HM Slaingai BM Slaine N Slaine ⁊ uaim Chruachan nó dearc Fearna *add.* H

43. Trí díthruib Hérenn: Fid Mór hi Cúailgni, Fid Déicsen hi Tuirtri, Fid Moithre hi Connachtaib.

dithreba BM Fid Dexin N

44. Trí dotcaid Hérenn: abbdaine Bendchuir, [A] abbdaine Lainne Ela, ríge Mugdorn Maigen.

dotchaid LHLec [A] .i. ar imad argain air L abdaine Sláne nó Colmain Ela BM Laind Ela BM

[Pg 5]
27. The ... of Ireland—Dairchaill.
28. The Stability of Ireland—Moville.
29. The Martyrdom of Ireland—Dulane.
30. The Reproach of Ireland—Cell Ruaid (Ruad's Church).[23]
[23]'Ruadan's Church,' L.
31. The Chastity of Ireland—Lynally.
32. The three places of Ireland to alight at: Derry, Taghmon, Kilmainham.
33. The three rent-paying places of Ireland: Clonard, Glendalough, Louth.
34. The three stone-buildings of Ireland: Armagh, Clonmacnois, Kildare.
35. The three fairs of Ireland: the fair of Teltown, the fair of Croghan, the fair of Colman Elo.
36. The three forts of Ireland: Dunseverick, Dun Cermna,[24] Cathir Conree.
[24]On the Old Head of Kinsale.
37. The three mountains of Ireland: Slieve Gua,[25] Slieve Mis, Slieve Cualann.[26]
[25]*i.e.* the Knockmealdown mountains.
[26]The Wicklow mountains.
38. The three heights of Ireland: Croagh Patrick, Ae Chualann,[27] Benn Boirche.[28]
[27]'The Liver ('Pap,' L.) of Cualu,' either the Great Sugarloaf or Lugnaquilla.
[28]*i.e.* Slieve Donard.
39. The three lakes of Ireland: Lough Neagh, Lough Ree, Lough Erne.
40. The three rivers of Ireland: the Shannon, the Boyne, the Bann.
41. The three plains of Ireland: the plain of Meath, Moylinny, Moy-Liffey.[29]
[29]*i.e.* the plain of Kildare.
42. The three dark places of Ireland: the cave of Knowth, the cave of Slaney, the cave of Ferns.
43. The three desert places of Ireland: Fid Mór (Great Wood) in Coolney, Fid Déicsen (Spy-wood) in Tuirtri,[30] the Wood of Moher in Connaught.
[30]The Húi Tuirtri were settled in the four baronies of Upper and Lower Antrim, and Upper and Lower Toome in county Antrim.
44. The three unlucky places of Ireland: the abbotship of Bangor, the abbotship of Lynally, the kingship of Mugdorn Maigen.[31]
[31]Now Cremorne barony, county Monaghan.

[Pg 6]
45. Trí huilc Hérenn: Crecraigi, Glasraigi, Benntraigi.
Grecraigi HBM
46. Trí cáemnai Hérenn: abbdaine Lusca, ríge trí Cúalann, secnabbóite Arda Macha.
ríge fer Cualann NL sechnap L segnab-i nArdmachai N
47. Trí trága Hérenn: Tráig Ruis Airgit, Tráig Ruis Téiti, Tráig Baili.
trachtai L
48. Trí hátha Hérenn: Áth Clíath, Áth Lúain, Áth Caille.
49. Trí sligid Hérenn: slige Dála, slige Asail, slige Midlúachra.
sligthi MSS
50. Trí belaige Hérenn: Belach Conglais, Belach Luimnig, Belach Duiblinne .i. Átha Clíath.

belaig L Conglaisi N Luimne N .i. Átha Clíath *om.* N

51. Trí drommanna Hérenn: Druimm Fingin, Druimm nDrobeoil, Druimm Leithe.

om. HBM

52. Trí maige Hérenn: Mag mBreg, Mag Crúachan, Mac Liphi.

53. Trí clúana Hérenn: Clúain Maic Nóis, Clúain Eois, Clúain Iraird.

54. Trí tellaige Hérenn: tellach Temrach, tellach Caisil, tellach Crúachan.

Temair Crúachu Caisel HBM

55. Trí hessa Hérenn: Ess Rúaid, Ess Danainne, Ess Maige.

56. Trí fothirbi Hérenn: Tír Rátha Laidcniáin, Slíab Commáin, Slíab Mancháin.

om. HBM fothairbe N

57. Trí tiprata Hérenn: Tipra na nDési, Tipra Húarbeoil, Tipra Úaráin Garaid.

tiubrai N tipra Cuirp N nDési HBM tipra Uarainn Garaid HBM t. Uaran nGarad N Breifene N tipra Braithcleasan Brigdi H Braichleasan Brigde BM

58. Trí haimréide Hérenn: Breifne, Bairenn, Bérre[A].

haimreid L Boirind M [A] Beandtraigi H

59. Trí hinbera Hérenn: Inber na mBárc, Inber Féile, Inber Túaige.

60. Trí hairderca Hérenn: Léimm Conculaind, Dún Cáin, Srub Brain.

hirrdraici H oirrdirc M

[Pg 7]

45. The three evil ones of Ireland: the Crecraige,[32] the Glasraige, the Benntraige.[33]

[32]A tribe settled in the barony of Coolavin, county Sligo, and in the adjacent part of county Roscommon.

[33]Either Bantry in county Cork, or Bantry in county Wexford.

46. The three comfortable places of Ireland: the abbotship of Lusk, the kingship of the three Cualu,[34] the vice-abbotship of Armagh.

[34]'Of the men of Cualu,' NL.

47. The three strands of Ireland: the strand of Ross Airgit,[35] the strand of Ross Teiti, the strand of Baile.[36]

[35]A territory in the barony of Upper Ormond, county Tipperary.

[36]Now Dundalk.

48. The three fords of Ireland: Ath Cliath (Hurdle-ford), Athlone (the Ford of Luan), Ath Caille (Wood-ford).[37]

[37]Perhaps Áth Caille Rúaide on the Shannon.

49. The three highroads of Ireland: Slige Dala,[38] Slige Asail, Slige Luachra.[39]

[38]The great south-western road from Tara into Ossory.

[39]A road running northward from Tara.

50. The three mountain-passes of Ireland: Baltinglass, the Pass of Limerick, the Pass of Dublin.

51. The three ridges of Ireland: Druim Fingin, Druim nDrobeoil, Druim Leithe.[40]

[40]In Breffny.

52. The three plains of Ireland: Moy Bray, Moy Croghan, Moy Liffey.

53. The three meadows of Ireland: Clonmacnois, Clones, Clonard.

54. The three households of Ireland: the household of Tara, the household of Cashel, the household of Croghan.

55. The three waterfalls of Ireland: Assaroe, Eas Danainne,[41] Eas Maige.

[41]On the Shannon opposite Dunass, co. Clare.

56. The three fields (?) of Ireland: the land of Rathlynan, Slieve Comman, Slieve Manchain.

57. The three wells of Ireland: the Well of the Desi, the Well of Uarbel,[42] the Well of Uaran Garaid.

[42]Probably near *Sescenn Uarbéoil* in Leinster (Mountseskenn?).

58. The three uneven places of Ireland: Breffny, the Burren, Beare.

59. The three estuaries of Ireland: Inver na mBarc,[43] Inver Feile,[44] Inver Tuaige.[45]

[43]*Dún na mBárc* is in Bantry Bay.

[44]The estuary of the Feale.

[45]'The axe-shaped estuary,' *i.e.* the mouth of the Bann.

60. The three conspicuous places of Ireland: Cuchulinn's Leap,[46] Dunquinn, Sruve Brain.[47]

[46]*i.e.* Loop Head.

[47]In the west of Kerry (i n-iarthar Hérenn, YBL. 123^{b31}).

[Pg 8]

61. Trí gnátha Hérenn: Tráig Lí, Lúachair Dedad, Slíab Fúait.

gnath N gnáith HM Líí N

62. Trí hamrai la Táin Bó Cúailnge: .i. in cuilmen dara héisi i nÉrinn; in marb dia haisnéis don bíu .i. Fergus mac Róig dia hinnisin do Ninníne éicius i n-aimsir Corbmaic maic Fáeláin; intí dia n-aisnéth*er*, coimge bliadna dó.

om. HBMLec coimde N

63. Trí meinistri fer Féne: .i. cích, grúad, glún.

64. Trí dotcaid duine: deog therc d'uisci, ítu i cormthig, suide cumang for achad.

dotchaid L dodcaid BM luige dige BM luige re dig H

65. Trí dotcaid threbtha: gort salach, iarmur cléithe, tech drithlennach.

dotchaid L dodcaid B iarmor B

66. Trí hairgarta ecalse: caillech fri clocc, athláech i n-apdaine, banna for altóir.

hairgairt L hairgair H hurgoirt B ina habdaine B bainne NM bæn̄ for a haltoir B

67. Trí fáilti co n-íarduibi: fer tochmairc, fer gaite, fer aisnéise.

fochmairc NHBMLec aisneidsi N

68. Trí bróin ata ferr fáilti: brón treóit oc ithe messa, brón guirt apaig, brón feda fo mess.

is ferr H ita ferr L at ferr N broin MB ac aipgiudud BM ig messrugud H

69. Trí fáilti ata messu brón: fáilti fir íar ndiupairt, fáilti fir íar luga eithig, fáilti fir íar fingail.

measum B iar ndiubairt N iar mbreith diubarta BM iar mbreith a dibirta H failte fir luga eithig B fir *om.* BM failte fir iar marbad a bráthar a[c] cosnom a ḟeraind fris BM

70. Trí fiada co n-anḟiad: gréss i n-óentig fri muintir, uisce rothé dar cosa, bíad goirt cen dig.

fiad L anbfiad N tri fiaidaichi ad mesa H greasa BM for cosaib HM dar cosaib NB biad goirt doib B

71. Trí dotcaid maic athaig: clemnas fri hócthigern, gabáil for tascor ríg, commaid fri meirlechu.

dotchaid L dodca d B hoigthigearna MN tarscur BM tascor (nó tarcor) N tairrseach (!) L

72. Trí dotcaid threbairi: tarcud do drochmnái, fognam do drochḟlaith, cóemchlód fri drochḟerann.

dodchaidh B targad BM drochlaith M drochlaech H claechlud H caemclodh M drochírind B

73. Trí búada trebairi: tarcud do degmnái, fognam do degḟlaith, cóemchlód fri dagḟerann.

[Pg 9]

trebtha N targad B deadlaech H claechmod H deigferand HM degthigern (!) B

61. The three familiar places[48] of Ireland: Tralee, Logher, the Fews.

[48]Or, perhaps, 'places of common resort.'

62. Three wonders concerning the Táin Bó Cúailnge; that the *cuilmen* came to Ireland in its stead; the dead relating it to the living, viz. Fergus mac Róig reciting it to Ninníne the poet in the time of Cormac mac Fáeláin; one year's protection to him to whom it is recited.

63. The three halidoms of the men of Ireland: breast, cheek, knee.

64. Three unfortunate things for a man: a scant drink of water, thirst in an ale-house, a narrow seat upon a field.

65. Three unfortunate things of husbandry: a dirty field, leavings of the hurdle, a house full of sparks.

66. Three forbidden things of a church: a nun as bellringer, a veteran in the abbotship, a drop upon the altar.

67. Three rejoicings followed by sorrow: a wooer's, a thief's, a tale-bearer's.

68. Three sorrows that are better than joy: the heaviness of a herd feeding on mast, the heaviness of a ripe field,[49] the heaviness of a wood under mast.

[49]'Of a ripening field,' BM.

69. Three rejoicings that are worse than sorrow: the joy of a man who has defrauded another, the joy of a man who has perjured himself, the joy of a man who has committed parricide.[50]

[50]'Of a man who has slain his brother in contesting his land,' BM.

70. The three worst welcomes: a handicraft in the same house with the inmates, scalding water upon the feet, salt food without a drink.

71. Three unfortunate things for the son of a peasant: marrying into the family of a franklin, attaching himself to the retinue of a king, consorting with thieves.

72. Three unfortunate things for a householder: proposing to a bad woman, serving a bad chief, exchanging for bad land.

73. Three excellent things for a householder: proposing to a good woman, serving a good chief, exchanging for good land.

[Pg 10]

74. Trí hóenaig eserte: célide hi tig gobann, célide hi tig ṡáir, dul do chennuch cen áirche.

hænaigi nasearta B neiseirti H haonaige neserte N esertai Lec airrdhe N

75. Trí cóil ata ferr folongat in mbith: cóil srithide hi folldeirb, cóil foichne for tuinn, cóil snáithe dar dorn dagmná.

foloingead imbith B is ferr isin mbith N sreibe LLec srithide B srithide foildeirb N

76. Trí duirn ata dech for bith: dorn degṡáir, dorn degmná, dorn deggobann.

for doman BM dorn sair dorn gabonn dorn daim N degdaim BM

77. Tréde conaittig fírinne: mess, tomus, cubus.

tri conaitig B

78. Tréde conaittig brethemnas: gáis, féige, fiss.

a tri conaitig B

79. Trí túarascbála étraid: osnad, cluiche, céilide.

osnaid N miad LBM

80. Tréde ara carthar escara: máin, cruth, innraccus.

a tri BM treidi H gnás alaig erlabra HM airdearcus B

81. Tréde ara miscnigther cara: fogal, dognas, dímainche.

treidi H a tri M tri L fogail H dimainecht HM

82. Trí buirb in betha: óc contibi sen, slán contibi galarach, gáeth contibi báeth.

contib BM contibe N gallrach BM gallrai N bæth contib gæth BM

83. Trí buidir in betha: robud do throich, airchisecht fri faigdech, cosc mná báithe do drúis.

urchuidme ria foidhech N ærcuidmed fri foigeaeh B mná druithi B

84. Trí cáin docelat éitchi: sobés la anricht, áne la dóer, ecna la dodelb.

doceilead eitig B handracht B dodealb B dodeilb N

85. Trí héitich docelat cáin: bó binnech cen as, ech án amlúath, sodelb cen tothucht.

doceiled BM beinnech N

86. Trí óible adannat seirc: gnúis, alaig, erlabra.

haibne adannaid searc B adanta serce N alaid N

87. Trí haithne co fomailt: aithne mná, aithne eich, aithne salainn.

haithneada Lec tomailt B ṡalainn L

88. Trí búada téiti: ben cháem, ech maith, cú lúath.

teite N buadnasa tétnai HBMLec

89. Trí ségainni Hérenn: fáthrann, adbann a cruit, berrad aigthe.

segaind M tri comartha segainn N segraind B Hérenn *om.* MB fatraind B fadbann N fadhbond MB aigthe *om.* BM a cruit *om.* MN

74. Three holidays[51] of a landless man[52]: visiting in the house of a blacksmith, visiting in the house of a carpenter, buying without bonds.

[51]Or, perhaps, 'fairs, foregatherings.'

[52]Or 'vagrant.'

75. Three slender things that best support the world: the slender stream of milk from the cow's dug into the pail, the slender blade of green corn upon the ground, the slender thread over the hand of a skilled woman.

76. Three hands that are best in the world: the hand of a good carpenter, the hand of a skilled woman, the hand of a good smith.

77. Three things which justice demands: judgment, measure, conscience.

78. Three things which judgment demands: wisdom, penetration, knowledge.

79. Three characteristics of concupiscence: sighing, playfulness,[53] visiting.

[53]Or 'dalliance.'

80. Three things for which an enemy is loved: wealth, beauty, worth.[54]

[54]'distinction,' B. 'familiarity, fame (leg. allad), speech,' H.

81. Three things for which a friend is hated: trespassing,[55] keeping aloof,[56]fecklessness.

[55]Or 'encroaching.'

[56]Literally, 'unfamiliarity.'

82. Three rude ones of the world: a youngster mocking an old man, a healthy person mocking an invalid, a wise man mocking a fool.

83. Three deaf ones of the world: warning to a doomed man, mocking[57] a beggar, keeping a loose woman from lust.

[57]'pitying,' L.

84. Three fair things that hide ugliness: good manners in the ill-favoured, skill in a serf, wisdom in the misshapen.

85. Three ugly things that hide fairness: a sweet-lowing cow without milk, a fine horse without speed, a fine person without substance.

86. Three sparks that kindle love: a face, demeanour, speech.

87. Three deposits with usufruct: depositing a woman, a horse, salt.

88. Three glories of a gathering: a beautiful wife, a good horse, a swift hound.

89. Three accomplishments of Ireland: a witty stave, a tune on the harp,[58] shaving a face.

[58]Literally, 'out of a harp.'

[Pg 12]

90. Trí comartha clúanaigi: búaidriud scél, cluiche tenn, abucht co n-imdergad.

tri comartha cluanaide N clu ænaigh M cluænaige B teinn L tind BM abocht HLec abhacht M co n-imnead nó imdergad HLec co n-uaithiss L co n-aitis N

91. Trí gena ata messu brón: gen snechta oc legad, gen do mná frit íar mbith ḟir aili lé, gen chon ḟoilmnich.

ad meassam HMB mesom L drochmna LN frit *om.* L iar fes le fer n-aili H iar mbeith fri araile BM foleimnighe N foilmig dot letrad H foleimnigh (foilmnig B) agud rochtain dott ithe MB

92. Trí báis ata ferr bethaid: bás iach, bás muicce méithe, bás foglada.

ad HBM beatha H iaich L bás iaich bás muici meithi bás fodhladlu L fogladai N fodalada B bás bithbenaig B luifenaich Lec

93. Trí húathaid ata ferr sochaidi: úathad dagbríathar, úathad bó hi feór, úathad carat im chuirm.

uath ada N ad M is H deagbriathar H degflaith MB

94. Trí brónaig choirmthige: fer dogní fleid, fer dia ndéntar, fer ibes menip sáithech

fleid *om.* B fer nostairbir H fer teid dia tairtiud minab saitheach M

95. Trí cuitbidi in domain: fer lonn, fer étaid, fer díbech.

cuidmidi H

96. Trí cuil túaithe: flaith brécach, breithem gúach, sacart colach.

flaitheamh BM sacart tuisledach N sagart diultach B diultadhach M

97. Trí fuiric thige degduni: cuirm, fothrucud, tene mór.

fuiric .i. fleadh nó féasta B daghduine N

98. Trí fuiric thige drochduni: debuid ar do chinn, athchosan frit, a chú dot gabáil.

achmusan NBM a cu dod ledrad N do congabail M drochscel lat immach L

99. Trí gretha tige degláich: grith fodla, grith suide, grith coṁéirge.

tri grith L tri gartha M fogla L suigidhe BM

100. Trí dorchæ ná dlegat mná do imthecht: dorcha cíach, dorcha aidche, dorcha feda.

nach dleguid N narfacad do mnai imteact B d'imtecht NM

101. Trí sailge boccachta: imgellad, immarbág, imreson.

soilge BM imgellad bag L imarbaid imreasain BM imarbaigh imressain N imreason nó imraichni L

102. Trí airisena boccachta: sírchéilide, sírdécsain, síriarfaige.

hærsenna BM hairisin N sirfiarfaighe M sirfiarfaigid N

[Pg 13]

90. Three ungentlemanly things: interrupting stories, a mischievous game, jesting so as to raise a blush.

91. Three smiles that are worse than sorrow: the smile of the snow as it melts, the smile of your wife[59] on you after another man has been with her,[60] the grin of a hound ready to leap at you.[61]

[59]'Of a bad woman,' LN.

[60]'After sleeping with another man,' H.

[61]'To tear you to pieces,' H. 'Coming up to devour you,' MB.

92. Three deaths that are better than life: the death of a salmon, the death of a fat pig, the death of a robber.[62]

[62]'Of a criminal,' B.

93. Three fewnesses that are better than plenty: a fewness of fine words, a fewness of cows in grass, a fewness of friends around ale.[63]

[63]'good ale,' MB.

94. Three sorrowful ones of an alehouse: the man who gives the feast, the man to whom it is given, the man who drinks without being satiated.[64]

[64]'Who goes to it unsatiated,' M. *i.e.* who drinks on an empty stomach.

95. Three laughing-stocks of the world: an angry man, a jealous man, a niggard.

96. Three ruins of a tribe: a lying chief, a false judge, a lustful[65] priest.

[65]'Stumbling, offending,' N. 'Fond of refusing,' B.

97. Three preparations of a good man's house: ale, a bath, a large fire.

98. Three preparations of a bad man's house: strife before you, complaining to you, his hound taking hold of you.[66]

[66]'Tearing you,' N. 'A bad story to speed you on your way,' L.

99. Three shouts of a good warrior's house: the shout of distribution, the shout of sitting down, the shout of rising up.

100. Three darknesses into which women should not go: the darkness of mist, the darkness of night, the darkness of a wood.

101. Three props of obstinacy[67]: pledging oneself, contending, wrangling.

102. Three characteristics of obstinacy[67]: long visits, staring, constant questioning.

[67]Literally, 'buckishness.'

[Pg 14]

103. Trí comartha meraigi: slicht a chíre ina ḟolt, slicht a ḟiacal ina chuit, slicht a luirge ina diaid.

comarthadha M meraigthe N 'na cend BM 'na cuit BM inandiaig B na diaidh M

104. Trí máidme clúanaigi: ató ar do scáth, rosaltrus fort, rotflinch*us* com étach.

cluainige BM ato BM atu L rodsaltar M rosaltrur ort L rosflinch*us* com edach N rofliuchus com ediuch BM comh edach L

105. Trí bí focherdat marbdili: oss foceird a congna, fid foceird a duille, cethra focerdat a mbrénḟinda.

om. BMHLec

106. Trí scenb Hérenn: Tulach na nEpscop, Ached Déo, Duma mBúirig.

om. BMHLec achad N

107. Trí hingnad Hérenn: lige inn abaic, lige nEothuili, allabair i foccus.

om. BMHLec hinganta N allubuir a fogus N

108. Trí daurthige Hérenn: daurthech Birra, daurthech Clúana Eidnech, daurthech Leithglinde.

om. BMHLec

109. Trí hingena berta miscais do míthocod: labra, lesca, anidna.

do mitocuid N do togud BM lesce N anidna N nemidna BM .i. esinrucas *add.* H

110. Trí hingena berta seirc do cháintocud: túa, éscuss, idnæ.

beres L berta seircce de caintogud BM serc N caintocaid N tri hadbair serci Lec tóa esces idna N esca BMLec

111. Trí túa ata ferr labra: túa fri forcital, túa fri hairfitiud, túa fri procept.

labrai N sproicept B sproicepht M fri aithfrend N

112. Trí labra ata ferr túa: ochán rig do chath, sreth immais, molad iar lúag.

uchan N ocon*n* BM hairfidiud *nó* fís BM luadh B

113. Trí hailgesa étúalaing .i. éirg cen co dechais, tuc cenitbé, déna ceni derna.

haisgeadha edualaing B erg gen cotis H tuc gen gud beirg (?) gen go gaemais dena gen go heda B tuca gen cobe N gen gudbe M gen [go] dernais N gen go feta HM

114. Trí hamaite bít[e] i ndrochthig óiged .i. sentrichem senchaillige, roschaullach ingine móile, sirite gillai.

hamaide drochtoighe BM sentriche caillige BM sentrichim N rosc cailleach ingine siridhe gillai BM siride N sirithe L

115. Trí hairig na ndúalche: sant, cráes, étrad.

[Pg 15]

103. Three signs of a fop: the track of his comb in his hair, the track of his teeth in his food, the track of his stick[68] behind him.

[68]Or 'cudgel.'

104. Three ungentlemanly boasts: I am on your track, I have trampled on you, I have wet you with my dress.

105. Three live ones that put away dead things: a deer shedding its horn, a wood shedding its leaves, cattle shedding their coat.[69]

[69]Literally, 'stinking hair.'

106. Three places of Ireland to make you start: Tulach na n-Escop,[70] Achad Deo,[71] Duma mBuirig.

[70]A hill near Kildare. See Thesaurus Palæo-hibernicus ii.. p. 335.

[71]At Tara. See Todd's *Irish Nennius*, p. 200.

107. Three wonders of Ireland: the grave of the dwarf,[72] the grave of Trawohelly,[73] an echo near.[74]

[72]Somewhere in the west (i n-iarthar Erenn, Fél., p. clvii).

[73]See Todd's *Irish Nennius*, p. 199, and Zeitschrift für Celt. Phil, v., p. 23.

[74]Nothing is known to me about this wonder.

108. Three oratories of Ireland: the oratory of Birr, the oratory of Clonenagh, the oratory of Leighlin.

109. Three maidens that bring hatred upon misfortune: talking, laziness, insincerity.

110. Three maidens that bring love to good fortune: silence, diligence, sincerity.

111. Three silences that are better than speech: silence during instruction, silence during music, silence during preaching.

112. Three speeches that are better than silence: inciting a king to battle, spreading knowledge (?),[75] praise after reward.[76]

[75]*Sreth immais*, which I have tentatively translated by 'spreading knowledge,' is used as a technical term in poetry for connecting all the words of a verse-line by alliteration, as e.g. *slatt, sacc, socc, simend, saland.* See Ir. Texte iii., p. 30.

[76]*Cf.* LL. 344*a*: Carpre asks Cormac what are the sweetest things he has heard, and Cormac answers: 'A shout of triumph after victory, praise after reward, the invitation of a fair woman to her pillow.'

113. Three impossible demands: go! though you cannot go, bring what you have not got, do what you cannot do.

114. Three idiots that are in a bad guest-house: the chronic cough of an old hag, a brainless tartar of a girl, a hobgoblin of a gillie.

115. The three chief sins: avarice, gluttony, lust.

[Pg 16]

116. Tréde neimthigedar crossán: rige óile, rige théighe, rige bronn.

117. Tréde neimthigedar círmaire: coimrith fri coin hi[c] cosnum chnáma, adarc reithi do dírgud dia anáil cen tenid, dichetal for ochtraig co rathochra a mbí ina íchtur for a úachtar do choñgna ⁊ cnámaib ⁊ adarcaib.

om. BMHLec dirge N otrach N corotochra N a mbid na hichtar N huachtar N congnaim N

118. Tréde nemthigedar sáer: dlúthud cen fomus, cen fescred, lúd lúadrinna, béimm fo chommus.

om. BMHLec tri ara neimit*er* N dluthugud N feiscre N ludh luaithreand N

119. Tréde neimthigedar liaig: dígallræ, díainme, comchissi ce*n* ainchiss.

om. BMHLec ara neimit*er* liagh N coimcisin gin ainces N

120. Tréde neimthigedar gobainn: bir Neithin, fulacht na Morrígna, inneóin in Dagda.

om. BMHLec ara neimit*er* gobaind N bir ndechin N

121. Tréde neimthigedar cerdai: fige ronn, cær comraic, plett for fæbur.

om. BMHLec cerd N flet N

122. Tréde neimthigedar cruitire: golltraige, gentraige, súantraige.

om. BMHLec

123. Tréde neimthigedar filid: immas forosna, teinm læda, dichetal di chennaib.

124. Dá mígairm míthocaid: commáidem do chétguine, do ben la fer n-aile.

atte dá ní igairm (!) do neoch .i. maidem a c*hét*guine ⁊ a bean do beith fri fer n-aill BM mitocaid N a cedgona N a ben la fer n-aile N

125. Teora airi[se]na iarnduba: comar, cocless, clemnas.

tri hairnadmand BMN iardubha M coicless LM coicle M

126. Trí bainne cétmuintire: bainne fola, bainne dér, bainne aillse.

banda NBM

127. Trí coiri bíte in cach dúini: coire érma, coire goriath, coire áiged.

core B duini L duine B goiriat N aitiu N notead B notheadh M

[Pg 17]

116. Three things that constitute a buffoon: blowing out his cheek, blowing out his satchel, blowing out his belly.

117. Three things that constitute a comb-maker: racing a hound in contending for a bone; straightening a ram's horn by his breath, without fire; chanting upon a dunghill so that all antlers and bones and horns that are below come to the top.

118. Three things that constitute a carpenter: joining together without calculating (?), without warping (?); agility with the compass; a well-measured stroke.

119. Three things that constitute a physician: a complete cure, leaving no blemish behind, a painless examination.

120. Three things that constitute a blacksmith: Nethin's spit, the cooking-hearth of the Morrigan, the Dagda's anvil.[77]

[77]For a description and pictures of these appliances, see YBL., p. 419*a*, and Egerton, 1782, fo. 46*a*.

121. Three things that constitute an artificer: weaving chains, a mosaic ball,[78] an edge upon a blade.

[78]O'Curry, Manners and Customs, ii., p. 253, thought that a *caer comraic* was 'a ball of convergent ribs or lines,' perhaps such a bead or ball of mosaic glass as is depicted in Joyce's *Social History of Ancient Ireland*, vol. ii., p. 32, fig. 171. *A cáer comraic* of eight different colours is mentioned in LB. 108*b* 20.

122. Three things that constitute a harper: a tune to make you cry, a tune to make you laugh, a tune to put you to sleep.[79]

[79]*Cf.* H. 3. 18, p. 87: tréide nemtighther cruit; goltraiges, gentraiges, suantraiges.

123. Three things that constitute a poet: 'knowledge that illumines,' '*teinm laeda*,'[80]improvisation.

[80]The names of various kinds of incantations. See Cormac's Glossary and Ancient Laws, s.v.

124. Two ominous cries of ill-luck: boasting of your first slaughter, and of your wife being with another man.

125. Three things betokening trouble: holding a plough-land in common, performing feats together, alliance in marriage.

126. Three drops of a wedded woman: a drop of blood, a tear-drop, a drop of sweat.

127. Three caldrons that are in every fort: the caldron of running, the caldron *goriath*,[81] the caldron of guests.

[81]Quite obscure to me. There is a heavily glossed poem in H. 3. 18, beginning*Coire goriath*. In H. 2. 15, p. 117b, after the colophon to Dúil Laithne (Goid.,2 p. 79), there are some further glosses, among which I find: goiriath .i. gardhamh in gach iath, erma .i. uasal-iompú no iar-iompa. But *érma*seems the genitive of *érim*, 'a course.'

[Pg 18]

128. Trí comartha láthraig bendachtan: clocc, salm, senad.

lathrach bennachtan H bendacht L senad NBMH ocsenad L

129. Trí comartha láthraig mallachtan: tromm, tradna, nenaid.

mallachtan HM neanad B neanntoch M tradnai BM tradna H

130. Teora muimmecha táide: caill, coim, adaig.

tri muime BM tri buime gaiti H coill HM

131. Teora ranna sluinte fri cáintocad: trumma, toicthiu, talchaire.

sloindti caintocaid N toicte N

132. Teora ranna sluinte dotcaid: tlás, áes, airbire.

dotcaid N tlass ois oirbire N

133. Dí derbšiair: tlás ⁊ trúaige.

siair L tlas ⁊ trousca N truaighe BMH

134. Dá derbráthair: tocad ⁊ brugaide.

brathair M toice ⁊ blailaige N togud B tacad H

135. Trí fuidb dotcadaig: ráthaiges, etargaire, fiadnaise. Dotoing dia fiadnaisi, íccaid dia ráthaiges, doberar béimm n-etaigaire ina chinn.

foidb dothcadaigh M toindid a fiadnaisi BM iccaid a rathaigecht beiridh builleadha etargaire ina cind BM.

136. Trí sethraeha góa: béss, dóig, toimtiu.

toimdi L

137. Trí bráthair uamain: sta! sit! coiste!

braitri N omain BM ist sta ⁊ coisde BM sta sit coist N

138. Trí mairb fortgellat for bíu: med, airmed, forrach.

forgellait H for fiu BM meid armeid BM forach H

139. Trí brothcáin rátha: rothicc, rosiacht, rotochtaig.

brothcain ratha N raithi L rodícc rosiacht roto*n*cai N

140. Trí dubthrebtha: tuga co fúatchai, imme co forṅgaire, tírad co n-aurgorad.

doidbtrebtai tugai co fodaib imed co forrngaire N tuighe go foidibh M co foitib Lec tiriudh M

141. Trí hiarnduba: fer tochmairc, fer gaite meirle, fer hic aisnéis.

fear fochairc Lec fer aisneisi N

142. Trí maic beres drús do lonnus: tuilféth, fidchell, dulsaine.

lundus N tulfeith N dullsaine L

143. Trí maic beres féile do ainmnit: grúss, rúss, rucca.

ainmned N grús rús rucad N

144. Trí maic beres neóit do deinmnait: crith, dochell, grith.

deinmnet N grith crith doicell N

145. Trí húar fíchte: tipra, muir, núæ corma.

huara N

146. Trí fúammann móaigthe: fúam bó mblecht, fúam cerdchæ, fúam aratbair.

fuamandu moaigti N moigthi L fuaim bo mblicht N

[Pg 19]

128. Three tokens of a blessed site: a bell, psalm-singing, a synod (of elders).

129. Three tokens of a cursed site: elder, a corncrake, nettles.[82]

[82]See my edition of *Cáin Adamnáin*, p. 13, note 3, and p. 38.

130. Three nurses of theft: a wood, a cloak, night.

131. Three qualities[83] that bespeak good fortune: self-importance, ..., self-will.

[83]Literally, 'parts.'

132. Three qualities[84] that bespeak misfortune: weariness, (premature) old age, reproachfulness.

[84]Literally, 'heaviness, weight.'

133. Two sisters: weariness and wretchedness.

134. Two brothers: prosperity and husbandry.

135. Three unlucky...:[85] guaranteeing, mediating, witnessing. The witness has to swear to his evidence, the guarantor has to pay for his security, the mediator gets a blow on his head.[86]

[85]The usual meanings of *fodb*, 'accoutrement, equipment, arms,' do not seem to suit here.

[86]Literally, 'the blow of mediation is dealt on his head.'

136. Three false sisters: 'perhaps,' 'may be,' 'I dare say.'

137. Three timid brothers: 'hush!' 'stop!' 'listen!'

138. Three dead things that give evidence on live things: a pair of scales, a bushel, a measuring-rod.

139. Three pottages of guaranteeing....[87]

[87]Obscure and probably corrupt. Cf. § 219.

140. Three black husbandries: thatching with stolen things,[88] putting up a fence with a proclamation of trespass, kiln-drying with scorching.

[88]'with sods,' NML, perperam.

141. Three after-sorrows: a wooer's, a thief's, a tale-bearer's.

142. Three sons whom folly bears to anger: frowning, ... ,[89] mockery (?).

[89]*fidchell*, the well-known game, gives no sense here.

143. Three sons whom generosity bears to patience: ... , blushing, shame.

144. Three sons whom churlishness bears to impatience: trembling, niggardliness, vociferation.

145. Three cold things that seethe: a well, the sea, new ale.

146. Three sounds of increase: the lowing of a cow in milk, the din of a smithy, the swish of a plough.

[Pg 20]

147. Trí hana antreinn: tipra i sléib, tene a liic, ana la fer calad.

luc MSS. anai la fear calaid N

148. Trí aithgine in domuin: brú mná, uth bó, ness gobann.

haitgine N aithgeinit L corathgen B coratgen M bru birite BM meas(!) BMLec

149. Trí diubarta forsná íada dílse: tinnscra mná, imthomailt lánamna, iarraid maicc.

hiad N imtomailt N iarr*aid* menicc(!) L

150. Trí cuir tintaiter do réir britheman: cor mná ⁊ micc ⁊ bothaich.

tinntaigter N

151. Trí nata[t] túalaing sainchuir: mac beo-athar, ben aurnadma, dóer flatha.

nad N

152. Trí maic nad rannat orbai: mac muini ⁊ aurlai ⁊ ingine fo thrilis.

erlai N

153. Trí ái nad eplet faill: ái dochuind, ⁊ dochraite, ⁊ anfis.

dochainn N docraite N

154. Trí fuile ná dlegat frecor: fuil catha, ⁊ eóit, ⁊ etargaire.

nad N etargaire N

155. Trí fuchachta nad increnat slabrai: a gabáil ar écin, a sleith tri mescai, a turtugud do ríg.

fúíchechta N slaibri N

156. Trí ná dlegat turbaidi: athchor maic, aicdi cherdai, gíallaigecht.

nad dlegait turbaid N aige cerda N

157. Trí aithne ná dlegat taisec: aithne n-écuind, ⁊ ardneimid ⁊ aithne fuirmeda.

haitne nad dlegait taisec N ecoind N fuirmidai L

158. Trí mairb direnaiter beoaib: aball, coll, fidnemed.

dorenatar beo N

159. Trí[ar] ná ditoing ná fortongar: ben, angar, amlabar.

dotoing na fortoing*er* L amlobar N

160. Trí ná dlegat athchommus: mac ⁊ a athair, ben ⁊ a céile, dóer ⁊ a thigerna.

na dlegait N

161. Trí nát fuigletar cia beith ar a ngáes: fer adgair ⁊ adgairther ⁊ focrenar fri breith.

nat fuigletar cia beit N fer adgair ⁊ adgair (sic) ⁊ adgairter ⁊ rocrenar N

162. Trí fors ná tuit aititiu 'na ré: bás, anfis, anfaitches.

anfuichc*h*es L anbaitces N

[Pg 21]

147. Three wealths in barren places: a well in a mountain, fire out of a stone, wealth in the possession of a hard man.

148. Three renovators of the world: the womb of woman, a cow's udder, a smith's moulding-block.

149. Three concealments upon which forfeiture does not close: a wife's dowry, the food of a married couple, a boy's foster-fee.

150. Three contracts that are reversed by the decision of a judge: the contracts of a woman, of a son, of a cottar.

151. Three that are incapable of special contracts[90]: a son whose father is alive, a betrothed woman, the serf of a chief.

[90]Or, 'of contracts on their own behalf.'

152. Three sons that do not share inheritance: a son begotten in a brake,[91] the son of a slave, the son of a girl still wearing tresses.

[91]Cf. the expression *meirdrech muine*, 'a bush-strumpet,' Laws v. 176, 4.

153. Three causes that do not die with neglect: the causes of an imbecile, and of oppression, and of ignorance.

154. Three bloodsheds that need not be impugned: the bloodshed of battle, of jealousy, of mediating.

155. Three cohabitations[92] that do not pay a marriage-portion: taking her by force, outraging her without her knowledge through drunkenness, her being violated by a king.

[92]*fuchacht*, or *fuichecht*, usually means 'cuckoldry,' a meaning which does not seem to suit here.

156. Three that are not entitled to exemption: restoring a son, the tools of an artificer, hostageship.

157. Three deposits that need not be returned: the deposits of an imbecile,[93] and of a high dignitary, and a fixed deposit.[94]

[93]*i.e.* a deposit made by an imbecile. *Cf.* Plato, Republic: "But surely you would never give back to a mad friend a sword which he had lent you?"

[94]But in the Heptads (Laws v. 196, 3) *aithne fuirmida*, there rendered by 'a deposited charge,' is enumerated as one of those to be restored even if there are no bonds to that effect.

158. Three dead ones that are paid for with living things: an apple-tree, a hazle-bush, a sacred grove.[95]

[95]there is nothing in the laws to explain this.

159. Three that neither swear nor are sworn: a woman, a son who does not support his father, a dumb person.

160. Three that are not entitled to renunciation of authority: a son and his father, a wife and her husband, a serf and his lord.

161. Three who do not adjudicate though they are possessed of wisdom: a man who sues, a man who is being sued, a man who is bribed to give judgment.

162. Three on whom acknowledgment does not fall in its time: death, ignorance, carelessness.

[Pg 22]

163. Trí foimrimme ná dlegad díre: homan, robud, toxal.

foimrime N foimrenn L na dlegaid N robad N

164. Trí duilgine conrannat gníaid: duilgine coiri, duilgine muilinn, duilgine tige.

duilcinne N conrenad gnia N

165. Trí nóill doná dlegar frithnóill: nóill mná fri húaitni, nóill fir mairb, nóill díthir.

naill nad dlegad fritnáill luige mna N luide N luige ditire N

166. Trí gráda coillte túath ina ngói: gói ríg, gói ṡenchada, gói bretheman.

om. HBMLec inango N go N

167. Trí sóir dogníat dóeru díb féin: tigerna renas a déiss, rígan téite co haithech, mac filed léces a cheird.

daoir dib fein N des N deissi L teid N treiges a cerd N

168. Trí ruip conberat duinechinaid: cú áraig, reithe lonn, ech daintech.

araid N reithid N daindtech N

169. Trí ruip ara tíagat cinta: cú foilm[n]ech, sleg caille, slissén chomneibi.

170. Trí imuserenat: saill, imm, iarn, fechemnas toisc leimmid eicsi.

imus crenait saill N sall L iaronn N feitemnus toisc leine im eiccsi N

171. Trí comartha aragella i tig britheman: ecna, aisnéis, intlecht.

comardda L aragellat a tig bretheman N taig L aisnesen intliuchtach L

172. Trí dlegat aurfocrai: aél coire, fidba cen ṡeim, ord cen dimosc.

dlegait urfogræ N fidbaigh can tseim ord gan dimosc N dinsem L

173. Trí doruis gúa: tacra fergach, fotha n-utmall n-eolais, aisnéis cen chuimni.

fothad utmall N eolus aisena oca*n* coimni N

174. Trí doruis a n-aichnither fír: frecra n-ainmnetach, ái fossad, sóud fri fíadnu.

an aithnit*er* fiorinne N freaccra n-ainmnedach N ainmeta L ai fosaid sodad N

175. Trí búada airechta: brithem cen fúasnad, etirchert cen écnach, coma cen diupairt.

fuasna L

176. Trí tonna cen gáissi: tacra calad, breth cen eolas, airecht labar.

ton*n*a gaisi N donnadgaissi L tonna gan gaoise H. 1. 11 brethem N

177. Trí búada insci: fosta, gáis, gairde.

buadad innsce N gois N

178. Trí cumtaig gáisse: immed n-eolais, lín fássach, dagaigni do airbirt.

lion fasaid N

[Pg 23]

163. Three usucaptions that are not entitled to a fine: fear, warning, asportation.

164. Three wages that labourers share: the wages of a caldron,[96] the wages of a mill, the wages of a house.

[96]*i.e.* of making a caldron, &c.

165. Three oaths that do not require fulfilment[97]: the oath of a woman in birth-pangs, the oath of a dead man, the oath of a landless man.

[97]Literally, 'a counter-oath, a second oath.'

166. Three ranks that ruin tribes in their falsehood: the falsehood of a king, of a historian, of a judge.

167. Three free ones that make slaves of themselves: a lord who sells his land, a queen who goes to a boor, a poet's son who abandons his (father's) craft.

168. Three brutes whose trespasses count as human crimes: a chained hound, a ferocious ram, a biting horse.

169. Three brutish things that atone for crimes: a leashed hound, a spike in a wood, a lath....[98]

[98]*comneibi* is a ἁπαξ λεγομενον to me.

170. Three things that ... salt-meat, butter, iron....[99]

171. Three signs that ... [99] in a judge's house: wisdom, information, intellect.

172. Three things that should be proclaimed: the flesh-fork of a caldron, a bill-hook without a rivet, a sledge-hammer without....[99]

[99]Obscure and probably corrupt.

173. Three doors of falsehood: an angry pleading, a shifting foundation of knowledge, giving information without memory.

174. Three doors through which truth is recognised: a patient answer, a firm pleading, appealing to witnesses.

175. Three glories of a gathering: a judge without perturbation, a decision without reviling, terms (agreed upon) without fraud.

176. Three waves without wisdom: hard pleading, judgment without knowledge, a talkative gathering.

177. Three glories of speech: steadiness, wisdom, brevity.

178. Three ornaments of wisdom: abundance of knowledge, a number of precedents, to employ a good counsel.

[Pg 24]

179. Trí miscena indsci: rigne, dlúithe, dulbaire.

miscne indsce N raighni L

180. Trí fostai dagbanais: fosta thengad ⁊ gensa ⁊ airnb*ern*tais.

fosta N fostadh tengad N airb*er*tais N

181. Trí fóindil drochbanais: fóindil scél ⁊ ataid ⁊ airberntais.

om. N

182. Trí búada étaig: maisse, clithcha, suthaine.

buadhad N cliche N

183. Trí ná dlegat othras: fer aslúi flaith ⁊ fini ⁊ fili.

nad d*leg*ait dire fer doslaig flaith ⁊ file ⁊ fine N feili L

184. Trí tharsuinn archuillet othras: echmuir, mil, saillti.

tharsunn L tarsuind aircaillti othiais N

185. Trí mná ná dlegat díri: ben lasma cuma cipé las fái, ben gatach, ben aupthach.

nat d*leg*ait N cia las f(a)oi N optach N

186. Trí dofortat cach flaith: góu, forsnaidm, fingal.

dofortad gach fl*ath*a N

187. Trí túarascbait cach ngenmnaide: fosta, féile, sobraide.

tuarascb*ál*a genmnaid fostad N

188. Trí ara n-aichnider cach fergach: ír, crith, imbánad.

tri aichnider L aranaithnent*ur* N hir L

189. Trí thúarascbait cach n-ainmnetach: sámtha, túa, imderead.

tuarascbalai gach nainmnedaigh samtad N tuai L

190. Trí thúarascbait cach n-úallach: mórthu, maisse, máine.

tuaruscbalai cach ndubalcai mortha N

191. Trí forindet cach n-umal: bochtatu, dínnime, humallóit.

forinded N bochtai N

192. Trí airdi gáisse: ainmne, faiscsiu, fáthaige.

hairdhe N faicsi fathaidhi N

193. Trí airdi drúisse: bág, imresain, condailbe.

om. N

194. Tréde immifoilnge gáis do báeth: ecna, fosta, sochoisce.

imfuilnge N

195. Tréde immifoilnge báis do gáeth: fúasnad, ferg, mesca.

imfailnge baoth N
196. Tréde faillsiges cach ndagḟeras: dán, gaisced, crésine.
cach degfer*us* N cresenai N
197. Tréde faillsigedar cach ndrochḟeras: serba, miscais, midlachas.
faillsigh*us* cach drochferus N
198. Trí foglúaiset fóenledchu: ingreim, dolud, dommatu.
fainnelca N dolai N

[Pg 25]
179. Three hateful things in speech: stiffness,[100] obscurity, a bad delivery.
[100]In Mod. Ir. *righneas labhartha* means 'an impediment in speech.' See Dinneen's Dictionary, s.v.
180. Three steadinesses of good womanhood: keeping a steady tongue, a steady chastity, and a steady housewifery.
181. Three strayings of bad womanhood: letting her tongue,[101] and ... and her housewifery go astray.
[101]Literally, 'stories.'
182. Three excellences of dress: elegance, comfort, lastingness.
183. Three that are not entitled to sick-maintenance: a man who absconds from his chief, from his family, from a poet.
184. Three sauces that spoil a sick-bed: ...,[102] honey, salt food.
[102]I believe *echmuir* to be the name of a plant: but I cannot find the reference.
185. Three women that are not entitled to a fine: a woman who does not care with whom she sleeps, a thievish woman, a sorceress.
186. Three things that ruin every chief: falsehood, overreaching, parricide.[103]
[103]Or rather 'murder of relations.'
187. Three things that characterise every chaste person: steadiness, modesty, sobriety.
188. Three things by which every angry person is known: an outburst of passion, trembling, growing pale.
189. Three things that characterise every patient person: repose, silence, blushing.
190. Three things that characterise every haughty person: pompousness, elegance, (display of) wealth.
191. Three things that tell every humble person: poverty, homeliness, servility.
192. Three signs of wisdom: patience, closeness, the gift of prophecy.
193. Three signs of folly: contention, wrangling, attachment (to everybody).
194. Three things that make a fool wise: learning, steadiness, docility.[104]
[104]*Cf.* dán ecna dogni ríg do bocht, dogni gáeth do báeth, &c., LL. 346ª35.
195. Three things that make a wise man foolish: quarrelling, anger, drunkenness.
196. Three things that show every good man: a special gift,[105] valour, piety.
[105]Such as art, poetry, &c.
197. Three things that show a bad man: bitterness, hatred, cowardice.
198. Three things that set waifs a-wandering: persecution, loss, poverty.

[Pg 26]
199. Trí slabrada hi cumregar clóine: cotach, ríagail, rechtge.
racht N
200. Trí all frisa timargar béscna: mainister, flaith, fine.
tri frisa N mineistir N flatha N

201. Trí caindle forosnat cach ndorcha: fír, aicned, ecna.

202. Tréde neimthigedar ríg: fonaidm ruirech, feis Temrach, roimse inna flaith.

tri aran*em*it*er* rí N

203. Trí glais foríadat rúine: náire, túa, dochta.

ruini L

204. Trí heochracha aroslicet imráitiu: mescca, tairisiu, serc.

oslaice imraite N

205. Trí orbai rannaiter fiad chomarbaib: orba drúith ⁊ orba dásachtaig ⁊ orba sin.

rannait fia comarbaoibh (*sic*) N

206. Trí seithir óited: tol, áilde, féile.

aide toil N

207. Trí seithir sentad: cnet, genas, éitche.

208. Trí seithir sognáise: feidle, soithnges, cuinnmíne.

feili soingtes connamno N soithgnes L

209. Trí seithir dognáise: luinne, cétludche, tairismige.

cetluithche N

210. Trí seithir sotcaid: sognas, sochell, súarcus.

sottch N sothchaidh L sognais L

211. Trí seithir sochlatad: léire, trebaire, rathmaire.

212. Trí seithir dochlatad: laxa, díbe, prapchaillte.

doclata N

213. Trí seithir ferge: écnach, augra, doithnges.

doingteas N

214. Trí seithir deirmiten: tromdatu, espatu, utmaille.

215. Trí seithir airmiten: torbatu, airétrumma, fosta.

216. Trí banlæ: lúan, mairt, cétáin. Mná co firu innib, bid mó a serc la firu indá serc a fer leo-som ⁊ beit a mná tar éis na fer sin.

bandla N at mna beit tara n-eiseiu N

217. Trí ferlæ: .i. dardáin, áine, domnach. Mná co firu intib, beitit na mná sin fo dígrad ⁊ beitit a fir dia n-éisi. Satharn im*morro* is laithe coitchenn. Is comlíth dóib. Lúan sáer do dul fri cach les.

aoine satharn *nó* domnach N innib N beidis N

218. Trí gníma rátha: fosta, féile, lobra. Fosta i n-árus, féile, arná ebra góe, lobra hícce .i. lécud a lomartha i n-indligud dar a fechimain.

om. ratha L lubrai N anarus N heibre gói N lubrai ice .i. leacadh lomartha anindlig*ed* dar cenn feichi*man* N

[Pg 27]

199. Three chains by which evil propensity is bound: a covenant, a (monastic) rule, law.

200. Three rocks to which lawful behaviour is tied: a monastery,[106] a chieftain, the family.

[106]'The credence-table,' N., perperam.

201. Three candles that illumine every darkness: truth, nature, knowledge.

202. Three things that constitute a king: a contract with (other) kings, the feast of Tara, abundance during his reign.

203. Three locks that lock up secrets: shame, silence, closeness.

204. Three keys that unlock thoughts: drunkenness, trustfulness, love.

205. Three inheritances that are divided in the presence of heirs: the inheritance of a jester, of a madman, and of an old man.

206. Three youthful sisters: desire, beauty, generosity.

207. Three aged sisters: groaning, chastity, ugliness.

208. Three well-bred sisters: constancy, well-spokenness, kindliness.

209. Three ill-bred sisters: fierceness, lustfulness, obduracy.

210. Three sisters of good fortune: good breeding, liberality, mirth.

211. Three sisters of good repute: diligence, prudence, bountifulness.

212. Three sisters of ill repute: inertness, grudging, closefistedness.

213. Three angry sisters: blasphemy, strife, foulmouthedness.

214. Three irreverent sisters: importunity, frivolity, flightiness.

215. Three reverent sisters: usefulness, an easy bearing, firmness.

216. Three woman-days: Monday, Tuesday, Wednesday. If women go to men on those days, the men will love them better than they the men, and the women will survive the men.

217. Three man-days: Thursday, Friday, Sunday. If women go to men on those days, they will not be loved, and their husbands will survive them. Saturday, however, is a common day. It is equally lucky to them. Monday is a free day to undertake any business.

218. Three duties of guarantorship: staying (at home), honesty, suffering (?); staying in one's residence, honesty lest he utter falsehood, suffering (?) payment, viz. letting oneself be stripped for an illegal action instead of the debtor.

[Pg 28]

219. Trí brothcháin rátha: éir[i]c nó thogním fecheman no díthechte.

brocain N *no* no thognim L ditechta N dithechdi L

220. Trí húais rátha ⁊ aitiri ⁊ nadma .i. dul fri dénam dúine ríg ⁊ daurthaige ⁊ choiri. Ar is úais do fir fine do thabairt fria céili.

eit*er*i N nadmadh fri N

221. Trí as anergnaid do neoch: slaide a eich ríana thigerna co salaig a étach, dul ina chocar cen gairm, a sírdéicsiu ina agaid oc caithem neich.

is ainergna N tri saineargnaidh M slaige BN rena BMN sirdeicsin N sirdegsain BM caithium BM aeaitniem a coda N

222. Trí bassa téchtai: bass etir a assa ⁊ a ochrai, bass etir a ó ⁊ a berrad, bass etir chorthair a léined ⁊ a glún.

corrthair M

223. Cia mesam hi trebod? Maic mná méile, fleda menci, clemna ile, immat meda scéo fína: notchrínat, ní thormaiget.

cidh is messa do treb*ad* ni *hansa* N mic B imad fianna nodcrinaid ⁊ nítoirmuigid BM imchiana (!) N nitormaigett N

224. Trí galair ata ferr sláinti: seola mná for mac, gríss bronn-galair glanas broinn, gríss timgaire olc dia maith.

seol N sceola(!) for fermac BM galar timargur olc do maith N timgaire B di maith B do maith M

225. Trí fáilti coirmthige: immed ⁊ dúthracht ⁊ elathó.

ealathaoi N ealado do neoch carthar BM

226. Trí fognama ata messam dogní duine: fognam do drochmnái ⁊ do drochthigerna ⁊ do drochgobainn.

mesa N drochflaith B drochf*er*ann N

227. Trí ata ferr i tig: daim, fir, béla.

dam N

228. Trí ata messum i tig: m*ai*c, mná, méile.

measum bite a taig mic BM

229. Trí comartha tirdachta .i. immargal ⁊ immarbág ⁊ meraichne.

im*ur*cal im*ur*baid imraithne N imabad LBM

230. Cenéle amus: salanaig buale ⁊ buicc brodnai ⁊ eóin erchoille ⁊ seiche corad.

cenela BM buale *om.* BM earcaille M córadh M

231. Cenéle dáileman: mórmenmnach meda, bolcsrónach brocóiti, itfa eserni, cúacroessach, donndabach, bolcra paitte, abartach escrai, geir grainne, cranndretel cuirn.

cenela BM metha H bolgsronach BM itfa eserne BM cuachroeasach BM cuachrochesach H baite BM haiti H abarthach easgraidh M gearr grandai B grenn graindi H crand rebartach H treiteal cuirnd M cuirnn L

[Pg 29]

219. The pottages of guarantorship: wer-geld or a debtor's ... or non-possession (?)[107]

[107]Obscure and probably corrupt. Cp. § 139.

220. Three things hard to guarantee and to become a hostage and to make a contract for: to go security for constructing the fort of a king, an oratory, and a caldron. For it is hard for a man of a family to be given with (?) his fellow.[108]

[108]I cannot make out the meaning of *doberim fri*.

221. Three things that are undignified for everyone: driving one's horse before one's lord so as to soil his dress, going to speak to him without being summoned, staring in his face as he is eating his food.

222. Three lawful handbreadths: a handbreadth between shoes and hose, a handbreadth between ear and hair, a handbreadth between the fringe of the tunic and the knee.

223. What is worst in a household? Sons of a bawd, frequent feasts, numerous alliances in marriages, abundance of mead and wine. They waste you and do not profit.

224. Three illnesses that are better than health: the lying-in of a woman with a male child, the fever of an abdominal disease that clears the bowels, a feverish passion to check evil by its good (?).

225. Three welcomes of an ale-house: plenty and kindliness and art.

226. Three services the worst that a man can serve: serving a bad woman, a bad lord, and a bad smith.[109]

[109]'bad land,' N.

227. Three things that are best in a house: oxen,[110] men, axes.

[110]'an ox,' N.

228. Three that are worst in a house: boys, women, lewdness.[111]

[111]'Or, perhaps, as in § 223, 'sons of a lewd woman,' only in that case we have no triad.

229. Three signs of boorishness: strife, and contention, and mistaking a person for another (?)[112]

[112]Or, perhaps, 'slight or superficial knowledge.'

230. Various kinds of mercenaries: ....[113]

231. Various kinds of dispensers: ....[113]

[113]As I could only offer unsatisfactory guess-work as a translation of these passages, I omit them altogether.

232. Trí as anso bís do accallaim .i. rí imma gabáil ⁊ Gall ina lúirig ⁊ athech do muin commairchi.

annsom (andso H) do agallaim bís BHM rig M cumairce N a chumairci H

233. Trí as mó menma bís .i. scolóc íar légad a ṡalm ⁊ gilla íar lécud a erraid úad ⁊ ingen íar ndénam mná dí.

trede BMHN scol*aigi* N scolaidi H íar lecun a eri uada H íar leccad a arad uad N

234. Cetharda forná bí cosc nó ríagail .i. gilla sacairt ⁊ cú muilleórach ⁊ mac bantrebthaige ⁊ gamain gamnaige.

fornach bi BM ná BM gamnaidhe M

235. Tri húais dóib: dul ar ríg nó úasal nemid, ar is lethiu enech ríg aidbriud; dul fri cath, ar ní túalaing nech glinni fri cath acht ríg lasmbíat secht túatha foa mám; dul fri cimmidecht acht nech lasa mbí mug dóer. Secht n-aurgarta dóib: dul ar deoraid, ar drúth ⁊ ar dásachtach, ar díaraig, ar angar, ar éconn, ar essconn. Imnedach da*no* cach ráth, ar is écen dí díanapud im cach ngell dob*eir*, aill riam, aill íarum.

n*em*i N it lethai L lethe N aidbriu N tulaing N glinde N acht nech laisimbiad N fo mam*m*i N cimbidheacht acht nech lasambiad mogh daor dil*es* N dasachtaig N imnedach do*no* cech raith N imni da*no* L dianapad N dobeir N

236. Trí hamra Glinne Dalláin i tír Eogain: torcc Dromma Leithe, is ass rochin ⁊ is dó-side forḟéimid Finn ní, co torchair im Maig Lii la aithech búi hic tírad, ut dixit Finn:

Ní mad biadsam ar cono. ní mad ríadsam ar n-echatan is aithechán átha. romarb torcc Dromma Letha.

Míl Leittreach Dalláin, cenn duine fair, dénam builc gobann olchena .i. ech usci robói isind loch i tóeb na cille, is hé dochúaid ar ingín in tṡacairt co ndergene in míl frie. Dam Dili in tres ingnad. Asind loch cétna táinic a athair co ndechaid for boin do búaib in brugad robói i fail na cille, co ndeirgenai in dam de.

as as rocin N forfeimdi N Muig Hi N Muig Hith H. 1.15 ma biasam N ma riadsim ar n-eacha N ricsam andechi L *Leth*æ N Leithi L ase docoid N fria N isin N co nderrna an dam fria N

232. Three that are most difficult to talk to: a king about his booty, a viking in his hauberk, a boor who is under patronage.

233. Three whose spirits are highest: a young scholar after having read his psalms, a youngster who has put on man's attire,[114] a maiden who has been made a woman.

[114]Literally, 'who has doffed his (boy's) clothes.'

234. Four on whom there is neither restraint nor rule: the servant of a priest, a miller's hound, a widow's son, and a stripper's calf.

235. Three hard things[115]: to go security on behalf of a king or highly privileged person, for a king's honour is wider than any claim; to go security for battle, for no one is capable of any security for a battle save a king under whose yoke are seven tribes; to go security for captivity, except one who owns a serf.

Seven prohibitions: to go security for an outlaw, for a jester and for a madman, for a person without bonds, for an unfilial person, for an imbecile, for one excommunicated. Troublesome moreover is every security, for it is necessary for it to give sudden notice as regards every pledge which he gives, now beforehand, now afterwards.

[115]I do not understand the force of *dóib*, 'to them,' either here or below after*secht n-aurgarta*.

236. Three wonders of Glenn Dallan[116] in Tirowen: the boar of Druim Leithe. It was born there, and Finn was unable to do aught against it, until it fell in Mag Li[117]by a peasant who was kiln-drying. Whence Finn said:

[116]Now Glencar, six miles to the north of the town of Sligo.

[117]The territory of the Tir Lí, west of the river Bann.

"Not well have we fed our hounds,Not well have we driven our horses,Since a little boor from a kilnHas killed the boar of Druim Leithe."

The Beast of Lettir Dallan. It has a human head and otherwise the shape of a smith's bellows. The water-horse which lived in the lake by the side of the church cohabited with the daughter of the priest and begot the beast upon her.

The Ox of Dil[118] is the third wonder. Its father came out of the same lake, and went upon one of the cows of the landholder who lived near the church, and begot the ox upon her.

[118]The oxen of Dil, daughter of Míl or Legmannair, are mentioned in the Dindsenchas, No. 44 and 111 (Rev. Celt. xv.).

[Pg 32]

237. Trí hamra Connacht: lige nÉothaili 'na thrácht. Comard hé frisin trácht. Intan atraig in muir, comard hé fria lán. Dirna (.i. cloch) in Dagdai, cia fochertar im-muir, cia berthair hi tech fo glass, dodeime a tiprait oca mbí. In dá chorr i n-Inis Cathaig, nocha légat corra aili leo inna n-insi ⁊ téit in banchorr isin fairrgi síar do duth, co tóet cona heisínib essi ⁊ nocon fagbat curaig eolus cia airm in doithi.

comaird i frisin lan N focerda a muir no cia bert*ar* N *no* do deime *no* dogeibt*er* a tibr*aid* oca mbid N do *nó* todeime L corr N chuirr L Ceitig N leigitt N do doich N heisenaib eisib ⁊ nochan fagbuid N eolus *om.* L hairm in doich N

238. Trí luchra ata mesa: luchra tuinde, luchra mná bóithe, luchra con foléimnige.

om. LHBM luchra duine H¹ foleimnigh N

239. Cisne trí ana soitcedach? Ní handsa són. Immarchor erlam, cuirm cen árus, cummairce for sét.

a tri N

240. Trí maic beres genas do gáis: gal, gart, gaire.

241. Trí airfite dála: drúth, fuirsire, oirce.

druith H¹

242. Trí ata ferr do ḟlaith: fír, síth, slóg.

adda H¹

243. Trí ata mesa do ḟlaith: lén, brath, míairle.

adda H¹ ada N

244. Ceithre báis breithe: a breith i ngó, a breith cen dilse, a breith cen ailig, a breith cen forus.

disle H¹ disliu N

245. Trí adcoillet gáis: anfis, doas, díchuimne.

a tri N ainbhḟes H¹ duas H¹

246. Trí muime ordain: delb cháin, cuimne maith, creisine.

ordan H¹ chaoin H¹

247. Trí muime menman: sotla, suirge, mesce.

socla .i. sochlú H¹

248. Cetheora miscne flatha: .i. fer báeth utmall, fer dóer dímáin. fer gúach esindraic, fer labor dísceoil; ar ní tabair labrai acht do chethrur: .i. fer cerda fri háir ⁊ molad, fer coimgni cuimnech fri haisnéis ⁊ scélugud, brethem fri bretha, sencha fri senchas.

249. Trí dorcha in betha: aithne, ráthaiges, altrom.

[Pg 33]

237. Three wonders of Connaught: the grave of Eothaile[119] on its strand. It is as high as the strand. When the sea rises, it is as high as the tide.

The stone of the Dagda. Though it be thrown into the sea, though it be put into a house under lock, ... out of the well at which it is.

The two herons in Scattery island. They let no other herons to them into the island, and the she-heron goes on the ocean westwards to hatch and returns thence with her young ones. And coracles have not discovered the place of hatching.

[119]*Cf.* § 197.

238. Three worst smiles: the smile of a wave, the smile of a lewd woman, the grin of a dog ready to leap.[120]

[120]*Cf.* § 91.

239. What are the three wealths of fortunate people? Not hard to tell. A ready conveyance(?), ale without a habitation(?), a safeguard upon the road.

240. Three sons whom chastity bears to wisdom: valour, generosity, laughter (filial piety?).

241. Three entertainers of a gathering: a jester, a juggler, a lap-dog.

242. Three things that are best for a chief: justice, peace, an army.

243. Three things that are worst for a chief: sloth, treachery, evil counsel.

244. The four deaths of judgment: to give it in falsehood, to give it without forfeiture, to give it without precedent, to give it without knowledge.

245. Three things that ruin wisdom: ignorance, inaccurate knowledge, forgetfulness.

246. Three nurses of dignity: a fine figure, a good memory, piety.

247. Three nurses of high spirits: pride, wooing, drunkenness.

248. Four hatreds of a chief: a silly flighty man, a slavish useless man, a lying dishonourable man, a talkative man who has no story to tell.[121] For a chief does not grant speech save to four: a poet for satire and praise, a chronicler of good memory for narration and story-telling, a judge for giving judgments, an historian for ancient lore.[122]

[121]*i.e.*, who has nothing worth hearing to say.

[122]See a similar passage in Ancient Laws i., p. 18, and in the tale called, 'The Conversion of Loegaire to the Faith' (Rev. Celt. iv., p. 165).

249. Three dark[123] things of the world: giving a thing into keeping, guaranteeing, fostering.

[123]*i.e.*, uncertain what will come of them.

[Pg 34]

250. Trí urgarta bíd: a chaithem cen altugud, a chaithem d'éis óiged, a chaithem réna thrath cóir.

haurgartho N[1] hurgairt HM hurghairrthe H[2] d'aithli aidead H cóir om. NH[2] iarna coir M

251. Cetheora aipgitre gáise: ainmne, sonmathe, sobraid[e], sothnges; ar is gáeth cach ainmnetach ⁊ sái cach somnath, fairsing cach sobraid, sochoisc cach sothengtha.

somna sobraicch H[2] sobés N soingthes H[2] somnoigh H[2] farsigh [*leg.* farsing] .i. sgaoiltech H[2]

252. Cetheora aipgitre báise: báithe, condailbe, imresan, doingthe.

253. Teora sírechta flatha: cuirmthech cen aisnéis, buiden cen erdonail, dírim cen chona.

airdanail N erdanail N[1]
254. Trí indchoisc ordain do duine: .i. sodelb, sáire, sulbaire.
a tri ina coisceadh ordan M suirbire H
255. Trí gúala doná fess fudomain: gúala flatha, gúala ecalse, gúala nemid filed.
dana H fodhomain M
256. Trí féich nach dlegar faill: féich thíre, duilgine achaid, argius aiste.
nat eple faill M aichid M argui*us* H

[Pg 35]

250. Three prohibitions of food: to eat it without giving thanks, to eat it before its proper time, to eat it after a guest.

251. Four elements[124] of wisdom: patience, docility, sobriety, well-spokenness; for every patient person is wise, and every docile person is a sage, every sober person is generous, every well-spoken person is tractable.

252. Four elements[124] of folly: silliness, bias, wrangling, foulmouthedness.

[124]Literally, 'alphabets.'

253. Three tabus of a chief: an ale-house without story-telling, a troop without a herald, a great company without wolfhounds.[125]

[125]This triad has been wrongly read (fais*cre* instead of fais*neis*) and rendered by O'Grady in his Catalogue of Ir. mss. in the British Museum, p. 91.

254. Three indications of dignity in a person: a fine figure, a free bearing, eloquence.

255. Three coffers whose depth is not known: the coffer of a chieftain, of the Church,[126] of a privileged poet.

[126]"Die Kirche hat einen guten Magen," Goethe, Faust.

256. Three debts which must not be neglected:[127] debts of land, payment of a field, instruction (?) of poetry.

[127]'Which do not die by neglect,' M.

[Pg 36]

GLOSSES AND NOTES

1. Gloss in H. 1. 15: oir gurab innte do bhí suidhe príomhaigh Éirenn.

2. .i. ordaighecht nó ord uaisle nó airechas .i. arduaislighecht tre adhluicedh na ríogh inte ⁊ na naoimh.

4. .i. serc Éirenn ó annsacht cháich uirre tre Muire na nGaodhal .i. Brighid.

5. .i. naomthacht tre naomaibh, nó foghluim sruth .i. saoi-raith.

7. .i. feronn buird riogh Éirenn.

11. .i. tre cáich innte nó tre n-iomad taisi innte.

13. .i. eircille ar grádhuibh dar ndóigh fa tuarasdul giolla foic[h]le, nó tuarastail.

14. .i. liodáin do gnáth.

15. .i. ealadhna mór ann ⁊ senchaoi ḟesa na sen.

16. .i. a n-iomat breithemhuin, nó cúirt, nó sgol féinechuis ann.

17. .i. ó iomad scol innte.

18. .i. aoibnes nó conách nó er tír fo sliocht Éireann.

19. .i. ag guidhe ar gach duine.

20. .i. tre leigen Temhrach. This refers to the curse pronounced by Ruadan, the founder of Lorrha, against King Diarmait and Tara.

22. .i. cairedh inte. St. Feichin, the founder of Fore, was famous for the austerity of his devotion. 'He used to set his wretched rib against the hard cell without raiment,' says Cuimmine in his poem on the Saints of Ireland (*Zeitschr.*, I., p. 63).

24. .i. diamharracht nó aon ar anacht nó gloine.

25. .i. luathghaire a mBreifne.

26. .i. grádh Dé.

28. .i. áit comhnuidhe.

30. .i. cill as mesa do cheallaibh nó béim aithesach nó ceall dáir.

31. .i. genmnacht.

32. .i. léime tara do tugsat.

33. .i. bailte bodaich.

34. trí clothra .i. coimhthineoil cluacha nó uirdherca.

36. Dún Sobairchi and Dún Cermna are, according to tradition, the oldest stone forts in Ireland, having been built by Sobairche and Cermna, who divided Ireland between them, about 1500 B.C., the former placing his dún in the extreme north, the latter in the extreme south on the Old Head of Kinsale.

37. Slíab Cua (or, by eclipse after the neuter *slíab*, Gúa), 'the hollow mountain,' or 'mountain of hollows' (*cúa* = Lat. *cavus*), the native name for the Knockmealdown mountains on the borders of Tipperary and Waterford.

42. Dercc Ferna was demolished by the Norse in 930. Hennessy, in a note on the entry in the AU., says that it is supposed to be the cave of Dunmore, not far from the city of Kilkenny, but adds "apparently on insufficient evidence."[Pg 37]

44. i. ionadha dona no nemhchonáig. Here we get the only gloss in L. Bangor is said to be unlucky, "because of its having been destroyed so often." It was frequently plundered by the Norse during the ninth century. As to the kingship of Mugdorn Maigen (now Cremorne barony, Co. Monaghan), it certainly was an ill-fated dynasty. Of the sixteen kings of this tribe who are mentioned in the Annals of Ulster, ten were put to death, of whom one (Suibne) was slain by his own brothers, while two brothers, Gilla Ciaráin and Máelmúaid, were slain within the same year (1020), the latter after having been king for but one day.

45. Beyond the fact that the three tribes here mentioned belonged to the *aithech-thuatha* or rent-paying tribes, I know nothing to throw light on the triad.

51. In Harl. 5280, p. 75a, marg. inf., Druimm nDrobeoil is said to derive its name from a horse called Drobel. (Ech Dedad. i. Drobel a ainm diatá Druim nDrob*eoil.*)

56. Here H. has the absurd etymological gloss futhairbhe .i. fothirbhe .i. tír mhaith na mbeo, nó ferann maith.

60. Léim Congcoluinn i gcondae in Chláir.

64. .i. miodhchonách duine. Suighe cumhang .i. deireoil.

65. iarmar cléithe .i. salchar na cléithe d'fágbhail a bferann. drithlennach .i. ferthain anuas nó linn thríd.

66. The first two items occur also in the list of proverbial sayings addressed by the Wizard Doctor to Mac Conglinne (*Aisl. Maic C.*, p. 73), with the significant variation that 'a veteran in the abbotship' has become 'a veteran in the bishop's chair,' showing that the 'Vision of Mac Conglinne' was composed at a time when the diocese had superseded the old monastic constitution. As to the 'drop upon the altar,' though O'Neachtain's gloss explains it as 'rain' (bainne .i. fer[th]uinn anuas), the Rev. Mr. O'Sullivan has furnished me with a much more likely explanation. He thinks it refers to the spilling of the consecrated wine from the chalice, which is considered a most unfortunate accident. No one but a priest is allowed to touch or remove it.

71. .i. tri donais mhic bodaigh. re óigthigerna .i. re duine uasal. for thascar rígh .i. céimionnadh móra do ghlacadh air (!) .i. do thabhairt uaidhe do striopach (!) .i. do thocaidhibh nó ar son gatuigechtadh.

72. targha .i. tineol no cruinnugadh .i. malairt ḟerainn mhaith ar dhrochferonn.

74. haonaighe nesairte .i. eisert .i. bochtain lag. gan airdhe .i. gan comhartha nó arra aige le gcennocha ní.

75. caol srithide a foilleirb .i. an sreab bainne da chrú .i. soidech. .i. fochan an gheamhair. for tuinn .i. faoi an cennar chroichin .i. ag denamh druithnechuis.

76. dorn daimh .i. cos ag treabhath.

77. mes .i. ó laimh. tomharas .i. ó ṡúil. cubhus .i. óna coimhesa .i. coimhfiosa.

79. eadruidh .i. adhaltraigh. cluithe .i. clesuighes. céilighe .i. cuairt.

80. maoin .i. tabhartus d'faghail uaide.[Pg 38]

81. dognas .i. nemhghnas. diomaoinche .i. díth maoine .i. do chuid do bhuain dhiod.

83. troich .i. do gerrṡaoghul. Cp. *Aisl. Maic Conglinne*, p. 71, 20.

84. áine la daor .i. saidhbrios ag daor neimhnidh .i. aithioch nó fer gan senchus. doidheilbh .i. duine grán[n]amh.

85. bó bennach gan eas .i. sreibh nó bainne. tothacht .i. gan tábhacht faoithe .i. tochus.

86. áibhle .i. splangca lasta grádha. aladh .i. hésa maith.

87. .i. trí ní curthar a ttaisge ara ccurtar caithemh. mná .i. taisge.

88. teidhe (*sic*) .i. aonaigh.

89. Seghaine .i. caomha nó séimhe. fáthrann .i. rann fáthach. adhbhann tri ciuil do ṡeinimh duine eile. berradh .i. eolus berr[th]a nó do bherrath go des. These three accomplishments were united in the person of Mac Díchóeme, the barber of King Eochaid with horse's ears (*Otia Merseiana*, III., p. 47), and in Donnbó (*Three Fragments*, p. 34, and Rev. Celt. 24, p. 44).

90. cluiche tenn .i. súgradh ten[n]. abhacht go n-aithis .i. súgradh le masla do thabairt.

91. .i. iar n-ealó óna fer féin. foileimnighe .i. chum do gerrtha .i. iar leigion sealga uaithe.

92. foghladha .i. gadaighe.

93. .i. trí haonarain is ferr ioná iomad. .i. begán do chaint mhaith. .i. ag ól fleadha nó sec[h]na imresain.

94. bróna .i. hamghaire. .i. deglaoch nach sáiseocha cách. .i. ga nderna ina ainim munath sásaigh[th]e é.

95. .i. faoi ndéntar magaid. lonn .i. fergach. éataigh .i. eudmhar. díbhach .i. doichleach.

99. gretha .i. garrtha. .i. gáir ag fodhail a mbídh. grith suidhe .i. chuman[n] bhídh. .i. ag éirghe ón mbiadh.

101. .i. postaidhe fir boigechta .i. boiggniomh. imgellad .i. síor-c[h]ur geallta. iomarbhaigh .i. comórtas. imresain .i. conspóidedha.

103. luirge .i. a bhata nó a mhná (lorg .i. ben, abhall, laoch, leo, arg).

104. da maoidhemh air féin gan nech da chur cuige.

105. os focherd a congan .i. fiadh chuires de a benna.

106. sceinbh .i. ionadha baoghlacha dochum sceinm do chur i neach nó ionada sccunamhla.

107. allabair .i. mac-alla nó iollabhar is gnáth a bhfod ó neach.

109. labra .i. iomad cainte. aimhiodhna .i. nemhgloine.

110. toa .i. bailbhe .i. éistecht. eiscis .i. escuidhecht. iodhna .i. glaine.

112. moladh iar luag .i. cennach tabhairt ar moladh.

113. .i. imthecht gion nach bhḟédann tú imthecht. .i. ní do thabhairt uaid na mbia agat. .i. gen go bfédann tú a dhénamh.

114. .i. senchaillioch triudhach casachtach ar aondhacht ann. .i. amhail cullach le buille ar choin, ar chat, ar mhada. .i. gach gránna siobharrtha 'na ghiolla.[Pg 39]

116. .i. a n-onoruighther nó uaislighther. .i. pluice ag síneadh a beoil. righe a bhronn .i. a bhuilg.

117. círmaire .i. 'fer dénta na gcíor. dichetal for otrach .i. adhbhal-cantainn le rosg nó orrtha. go rothochra .i. go docuiredh.

118. dlughughadh .i. cnesughadh. freiscre .i. frisearadh gan sergadh. lúth tar luaitbrenn .i. for a tighibh nó templuibh .i. rennaigheacht do cuiredh sa luaith. béim fo chumas .i. buille a coimhmheiseamnuighe féin.

119. dighalra .i. leighios iomlán na ngalar. diainmhe .i. gan ainiomh d' fágail iar genedhuibh. .i. coimhḟécsin nó fíoradharc.

120. .i. bior dobheir sásadh as gach ní rachad fair.

121. caer comraic .i. raed cruinn go ccomhtharrachtain d'iomat dath ann. fleath for faobhar .i. faobhar for faobhar.

122. cruitire .i. cláirseoir.

125. comar .i. docum treabtha nó coimhghélsine.

131. truime .i. tromdhacht. toice .i. saidhbhres. talchaire .i. toil charthanach ag gach duine do.

132. .i. tri neithe aisnéisi an doconáigh.

133. tlás [.i.] doní an trosgadh an duine tláit[h].

135. .i. cnapáin mísénamhla nó nemhconáigh.

139. trí brothc[h]áin rátha .i. trí neithe breithemhnuighther nó caoinbherthar ar antí théid a ráithiges nó a n-urrughas. roitioc .i. íocaidh na fiacha. rosiacht .i. éigion do nech do leanamhuin. rotho*cht* .i. ⁊ mionnughadh 'sa gcúis.

140. tugha go bhḟóidibh .i. fóide os toighe ar tech. imme go bfoighnagare (sic) .i. fál ⁊ fíoriongaire maille ris. .i. go ngoradh gér cloch a ndiaigh gortath na hátha.

141. trí fáilte go n-iarnduibhe. fer gaide .i. an tan bhíos da chrochadh. .i. doní faisnéis.

142. tulfeaith (*sic*) .i. drúis .i. toil féithe. dulsaine .i. cáinedh no cáinseoireacht.

143. grís .i. imdhergadh. rus .i. roifios. ruccaidh .i. ancroidhe.

145. nua corma .i. braitlis.

146. moaighthe .i. médaighthe sochair do neoch.

147. teine a lucc (!) .i. [a] tteallach. næ la fer calaigh (!) .i. naomhóg, coite, bád, long, do dhuine le purt.

148. aithgionta .i. neithe dobheir aithghin tarais no aithgini uatha. nes gabhann .i. mála cré.

149. .i. neithe ann a ttabhair neach iomarcaith naith ⁊ nach iadhann dísle orrtha ó nech dar ben iad. iarraid mic .i. luach oileamhna.

151. aurnadhma .i. pósta.[Pg 40]

153. .i. trí cúisi nach básaighenn d'faill do dhénamh umpa iad eibiulait .i. básaighenn. dochraidhe .i. duine díochairdigh.

155. slabhra .i. imdhergtha .i. pecughadh le mnái neich gan coibhche do dhíol ionnta, nach gcennuighther le airnéis nó éiric do díol ionnta. .i. coimhéigniughadh do rígh.

156. turbhadh .i. cairde d'iarraigh da ccur amach .i. da ttabhairt amach. .i. da athair tar éis altroma. .i. tar éis anbhaill do dhénamh a thabhairt da sealbhaightheoir. .i. braighe do tabhairt as láimh le comhall síotha.

157. .i. taisce do fúigfidhe ag égciallaidh. .i. do fuigfidhe ag duine mór. aithne formeda .i. do fuigfidhe gan aithne do thabhairt go cinnte i ccumhdach acht go héccinte air.

158. dorenathar bí .i. nech eirnighther no híocthar le beo do thabhairt da gcenn. fidnemed .i. coill ar a bhfuil neimhṡenchus nó atá da gcumhdach la huasal.

159. Trí ná dotoing ná fortongar. angar .i. mac ionghar nach bhfoghann da senoir do réir a dhualgais.

160. athchumas .i. do ghlacadh orra na athchomhasan (no do thabhairt daibh) (.i. ar a ceile).

161. .i. nach teighther faoi a bhfuigheall .i. a mbreitheamnuis. .i. cia do bheithdaois glic. fer adgair (.i. cu rios fios ort) agas adghairther (.i. an fer ar a gcuirther fios) agas ro crenair ria breith (.i. agas cennuighther mar breithemh le bríb le haghaidh breithe).

162. aitide .i. aonta. ainbhfaitches.

163. Trí fo imrime ná dleagaid (.i. imthechta amhuil ar marcuigheght) dire (.i. dire enecluise). toxal .i. tóccbhail agus ag dénamh athghabála.

164. duilchinn.

165. Trí naoill .i. luighe nó mionna nach cóir mhionnughadh 'na n-aghaidh. fir mairb .i. do bheith le bás go cinnte. ditire .i. do thréig a thír .i. do chur cúram an tṡaoighil de.

166. .i. céimionna mhilleas an tuaith le bréig.

167. renus a dheis .i. a dhúthaigh nó a feronn .i. bodach é ⁊ ní bhḟuil ced sencuis air.

168. For *comberat* H[1] has *conrannat.* dainntech .i. gremannach nó buailtech.

170. feichemhnas .i. lucht tagartha nó oificc na bhḟeithemhan. toisc. leimim. eicsi .i. muna foghluma.

171. aradgeallad. breithemhuin .i. fuasglais neach.

172. urfogradh .i. air ar coir miothaithnemh. ael coire .i. ag tógbhail feola coiri. fiodhbhaigh gan tseinm .i. meileg gan semann no thairn[g]e da chengal. ord ghabhan[n] gan dinesc gan tairn[g]e annsa bpoll .i. díon ina eis.

173. fotha utmhall gan eolus .i. bunadhas gan forus acht haimhnech, utmhall .i. roluath.[Pg 41]

174. soadh fri fiadnaib .i. iompodh a n-aghaidh na bhfiadhan do haondaighe.

175. breithemh gan ḟuasna .i. techt 'na aghaidh. eidirchert gan éaccnach .i. breithemhnas gan idhiomradh 'na dhiaigh. comha gan diubhairt .i. gan bhreith do bhreith le caomhmha nó gan leatrom aonroinn.

176. Trí tonna gan gaoise .i. do chuires anfa ar ghaois .i. gliocas.

177. fostadh .i. foisdinecht. gairde .i. athchumairecht.

179. .i. cúisi far cóir mioscuis don urlabhra. dlúithe .i. ar muin a chéile.

180. fostadh .i. na tengan 'na sost. airnbertais .i. ag dénamh ⁊ ag ordughadh gach neithe mar as dú.

182. maise .i. bregha. clithighe .i. bheith clithar.

183. trí ná dleaghaidh dire .i. truaighe nó comairce. .i. ealaighes ó flaith. agas file .i. ó eglais (!).

184. .i. trí hanlain[n] chrosta don othar. each .i. feoil eich. muir .i. míl mhoir .i. cointinn ar coinntinn.

186. Instead of *forsnaidm*, H. 1. 15 has forran .i. fírbrised.

187. sobhraidhe .i. brígh maith nó láidir.

188. ír .i. fer[g].

189. sam (*sic*) .i. anmhuin go socair. tua .i. socht nó éistecht. imdhergadh .i. gríosadh nó náire.

190. mórt[h]a .i. mórthacht. maise .i. maisech lais féin. maoine .i. a mhes gurab maoineach é.

191. forindet .i. doní faisnéis ar in umhal. dinmhe .i. dith inmbe.

192. faicse (sic) .i. meabair maith. fáthaidhe .i. bheith foghluma fáith-chialluigh.

195. fuasnadh .i. imresan.

196. cach ndagferas .i. guch feidhm nó gníomh iomlán nó feramhuil.

197. serbha .i. goid.

198. .i. docuires chum siubhail iad fainealca. ingreim .i. do ṡlad nó da gcrechadh. dola .i. da ngremughadh. domata .i. boichtecht.

200. fine .i. iomad fine nó móirmhes an fine.

202. fornaidm ruirioch .i. ríogha eile congbhail faoi. roimhse .i. roimhes nó torad mór ina ḟlaith.

203. tua .i. bailbhe. dochta .i. éistecht (!).

204. tairisamh .i. coimhniughadh alfaire neich.

205. .i. i bhḟiadhnuise na gcomharcadh. .i. daoine gan chéill .i. daoine ag imthecht le gaoith.

207. éitche .i. gráinche.

208. soingthes .i. urlabhradh mhaith. connamhna .i. coma degmhana nó de[g]mianadh.[Pg 42]

209. luinne .i. fergaighe. cétludche .i. cédluath ghaire. tairismidhe .i. iomarcraidh griaidh da chur a gcéill .i. tairismidhe.

210. sognas .i. goma maith le a ghnáthugadh. soicheall .i. goma soichellach nó luathghairech.

211. .i. trí 'ga mbíonn clú maith. trebaire .i. gliocas. rathmaire .i. rath mór do techt air nó bhfás fair.

212. dochlatad .i. miochluid. laxa .i. faillidhe. prapcaillte .i. a bheith cruaidh ⁊ luath .i. bheith caillte anna chuid go luath.

213. ecnach .i. ithiomradh. doingthes .i. droichtengadh.

214. deirmiten .i. athairmhidin. easpata .i. diomhaoines.

216. .i. trí laithe as sona do mhnáibh pósta. mná go fiora .i. mná do thabhairt chum pósta. .i. biadh na mná beo 'na ndiaidh.

217. fri gach leas .i. gach neithe bhus leas dó.

218. rátha .i. urradha. fostadh .i. comhnuidhe. féile .i. náire. lomradh .i. ag lomairt ag díol fiachadh. fostodha a n-arus .i. comhnuidhe a bpriosún lomradh íce .i. da lomairt féin ag díol fiachadh nó fulang é féin do lomradh do réir dlighe .i. leigen lomartha an dlighe dar cenn feichemhan.

219. eiric no toghniomh feichemhan (.i. an t-íoc do dhénamh darcenn a bhiodhbha) no dithecht.

220. .i. trí neithe as anfæ (leg. ansa) nó as doiligh dhaibh. .i. dol a n-urrudhas dún righ do dhénamh, decair sin. coire .i. coire longan. .i. do thabhairt an urrudhas re cechtar doibh sin aroile do dhénamh.

221. trí as ainer[g]na (.i. neimhealadhanta) do neach. .i. no go salaighenn a eudach do scarduibh.

222. ochradh .i. alt. berradh .i. mullach a chinn.

223. mic .i. iomad mac. mná .i. iomad ban. méile .i. amadan. cleamhna ile imchiana .i. iomad clemhnas a gcéin. notcrionad (.i. dibrid) agus ní thormaighid (.i. ní mhédaighid a tighes).

224. seol mná for mac .i. luighe seola. gris bronn .i. tesuighecht. galar tiomargar olc .i. togbhus an t-olc ⁊ ḟágbhus an mhaith 'na háit féin.

225. .i. gar cóir fáilte rompa, no dobheir an ḟáilte a ttigh fleadha im duthracht ⁊ ealatha .i. ealadha do thaisbeana[dh].

227. daimh. bealai .i. tuadh, biail.

229. tiordhachta .i. tuathamhlacht no bodamhlacht. iomargal .i. ime ro mheraighe focal. iomarbhaidh .i. comartus gníomh. meraigecht .i. mire.

230-231. omitted in H. 2. 15.

232. rí ima gabhail .i. im geall nó chreich. aithech do mhuin coimeirce .i. bodach ar a mbeith dhó ar coimeirce, nó tenn ar chúl aige.

233. .i. scolaire iar gcriochnughadh a leighen .i. iar leagha nó egluisech iar ndénamh ornaidhe. iar leaccad a araidhechta uadh .i. iar ccriochnughadh a term a nó aimsire.[Pg 43]

235. trí huais doibh .i. gar doilge doibh. .i. a n-urrdhas ar righ, ar esbog do bhrigh a leithe eneaclann an righ, nó inté atá na cronughadh ann. dul fri cath .i. dul a n-urrughas le cur catha. fri cimidh .i. dul a n-urrughas le brughaidh nó le siothcain. .i. secht neithe crosta donté rachadh a n-urrughas orra. dol ar dheoruighe .i. dol a n-urrughas. ar dhiaraigh .i. gan árus no coimhnaidhe aige. ar druith .i. duine gan céill, ar dhiaraigh .i. nach feidir árach air. ar angar .i. mac iongar. ar esccong (!) .i. senoir iar ndul a chéille uaidh. imnedhach dona gacha ráth (imṡníomhach go fírinnech gach urrughas díobh sin), .i. fulang dianbhás no dianollmhughadh no urfogra fa gach gealla dobheir aill ria n-aill iaromh .i. mionna a n-aghaidh mionn an ḟir oile .i. nach decha sé a n-urrudhas no le díola.

236. ag tioradh .i. ag goradh arbha.

238. luchra .i. gaire nó genamh.

239. .i. cia hiat na trí sonais dogheibh an duine sonadh? Ní handsa son .i. ní hainbhḟesach misi ar sin. iomarchor .i. iomchar. cuirm gan ára .i. deoch gan tech aige. .i. ar an tslighe go teghmaisech.

240. gaire .i. gaire maith.

241. .i. do ní oirfide nó comhluadar i gcomhdáil. druith .i. amatán. foirsire abhlóir nó ursoire. oircc (*sic*) .i. mesan nó cú beg.

243. léan .i. amhgar. brath .i. ar comarsan.

244. a breith a ngó .i. gúbreith brégach. gan disle .i. faoi omhan gan árach. gan ailic .i. gan hailche 'na timchioll .i. rosg ⁊ fasach.

246. duas .i. droichḟios.

247. socla (*sic*) .i. sochlú. suirge .i. le mnáibh.

248. .i. ceitheora da ttugann flaith mioscais nó nemhdhúil. baoth .i. leamh. uttmhall .i. roluath. fer labhar disceoil .i. labharrach cainntech gan sceol aige. fer coimhghne cuimhnech .i. go caoimhegna ⁊ cuimhne senchusa.

251. somna .i. so-omhnach .i. so-eglach (!). sobraicch .i. sobríoghach.

252. condailbhe .i. bághach nó leathtaobhach. doingthe .i. doitenguighe.

253. trí sirrechta flatha .i. suthainghesa nó neithe bhíos toirmisc ar uasal. .i. fleadha gan ealadha da ḟaisnéis. .i. cuitechta gan donail píobaire 'na tosach.[Pg 44]

[Pg 45]

INDEX LOCORUM

- Ached Déo, 106.
- Ae Chúalann, 38.
- Ardmacha *Armagh*, 1, 34, 46.
- Ard mBreccáin *Ardbrackan*, 23.
- Ath Caille, 48.

- Ath Clíath Duiblinne, 48, 50.
- Ath Lúain *Athlone*, 48.
- Bairenn *the Burren*, 58.
- Banna *the Bann*, 40.
- Belach Conglais *Baltinglass*, 50.
- Belach Duiblinne, 50.
- Belach Luimnig, 50.
- Bennchor *Bangor*, 5, 44.
- Benn mBoirchi *Slieve Donard*, 38.
- Benntraige *Bantry*, 45.
- Bérre *Beare*, 58.
- Birra *Birr*, 108.
- Bóand *the Boyne*, 40.
- Braichlesan Brigde, 57.
- Breifne, 58.
- Caisel *Cashel*, 54.
- Cathair Chonrúi, 36.
- Cell Dara *Kildare*, 4, 34.
- Cell Maignenn *Kilmainham*, 32.
- Cell Rúaid, 30.
- Cenannus *Kells*, 7.
- Clúain Eidnech *Clonenagh*, 108.
- Clúain Eois *Clones*, 53.
- Clúain Ferta Brénainn *Clonfert*, 19.
- Clúain Iraird *Clonard*, 3, 33, 53.
- Clúain Maic Nóis *Clonmacnois*, 2, 34, 53.
- Clúain Úama *Cloyne*, 12.
- Connacht, 43, 237.
- Corcach *Cork*, 16.
- Crecraige, 43.[TN 45]
- Crúachán Aigli *Croagh Patrick*, 38.
- Crúachu *Croghan*, 35, 54.
- Cúailgne *Coolney*, 43, 62.
- Cúalu, 46.
- Dairchaill, 27.
- Daire Calgaig *Derry*, 32.
- Derc Ferna, 42.
- Druimm Fingin, 51.
    - In Munster, famous for its fertility. See LL. 15[a] 11.
- Druimm Lethan *Drumlane*, 25.
- Druimm nDrobeóil, 51.
- Druimm Leithe, 51, 236.
- Dublinn *Dublin*, 50.
- Duma mBúrig, 106.

- Dún Cáin *Dunquin*, 60.
- Dún Cermna, 36.
- Dún Dá Lethglas *Downpatrick*, 26.
- Dún Sobairche *Dunseverick*, 36.
- Ess Danainne, 55.
- Ess Maige, 55.
- Ess Rúaid *Assaroe*, 55.
- Fid Déicsen i Tuirtri, 43.
- Fid Moithre i Connachtaib, 43.
- Fid Mór i Cúailgni, 43.
- Findglais *Finglas*, 8.
- Fobur Féichín *Fore*, 22.
- Glasraige, 45.
- Glenn Dá Locha *Glendalough*, 11, 33.
- Glenn Dalláin *Glencar*, 236.
- Imblech Ibair *Emly*, 15.
- Inber Féile, 59.
- Inber na mBárc, 59.
- Inber Túaige, 59.
- Inis Cathaig *Scattery Island*, 10, 237.

[Pg 46]

- Lann Ela *Lynally*, 31, 44.
- Léimm Conculainn *Loop Head*, 60.
- Leithglend *Leighlin*, 108.
- Less Mór *Lismore*, 14.
- Lettir Dalláin, 236.
- Loch nEchach *Lough Neagh*, 39.
- Loch nErni *Lough Erne*, 39.
- Loch Rí *Lough Ree*, 39.
- Lothra *Lorrha*, 20.
- Lúachair Dedad *Logher*, 61.
- Lugbad *Louth*, 33.
- Luimnech *Limerick*, 50.
- Lusca *Lusk*, 6, 46.
- Mag Crúachan, 52.
- Mag mBile *Moville*, 28.
- Mag mBreg, 52.
- Mag Lí, 236.
- Mag Lifi, 41, 52.
- Mag Line, 41.
- Mag Midi, 41.
- Mugdorn Maigen *Cremorne barony*, 44.
- Ráith mBoth *Raphoe*, 25.
- Ráith Laidcniáin *Rathlynan*, 56.

- Ross Ailithre *Roscarbery*, 17.
- Ross Commáin *Roscommon*, 24.
- Sinann *the Shannon*, 40.
- Sláine *Slane*, 21.
- Slíab Commáin, 56.
- Slíab Cúa, 37.
- Slíab Cúalann, 37.
- Slíab Fúait *the Fews*, 61.
- Slíab Mancháin, 56.
- Slíab Mis, 37.
- Slige Assail, 9, 49.
- Slige Dála, 49.
- Slige Midlúachra, 49.
- Srub Brain, 60.
- Tailtiu *Teltown*, 35.
- Tamlachta *Tallaght*, 8.
- Tech Cairnig, 9.
- Tech Munna *Taghmon*, 32.
- Temair *Tara*; gen. Temrach 54, 202.
- Tipra Cuirp, 57.
    - See Tog. Br. Dá Derga § 154, YBL.
- Tipra na nDési, 57.
- Tipra Uaráin Garaid, 57.
- Tipra Uarbeóil, 57.
- Tír Dá Glas *Terryglas*, 18.
- Tír Eogain *Tirowen*, 236.
- Tráig Baili, 47.
- Tráig Lí *Tralee*, 61.
- Tráig Ruis Airgit, 47.
- Tráig Ruis Téiti, 47.
- Tuirtri, 43.
- Tulach na nEpscop, 106.
- Tulen *Dulane*, 29.
- Uam Chnogba *Knowth*, 42.
- Uam Slángæ *Slaney*, 42.

INDEX NOMINUM

- Colmán Ela, 35.
- Corbmac mac Fáeláin, 62.
- in Dagda 120, 237.
- Dil, 236.
- Eothaile, 107, 237.
- Fergus mac Róich, 62.
- Finn, 236.

- Morrígan, 120.
- Neithin, 120.
- Ninníne éces, 62.

[Pg 47]

GLOSSARY

abartach, from abairt, *practice, feat*, a. escrai 231.
abucht (abocht, abacht) *a joke, jest* 90.
adbann *a strain of music* 89. With prothetic f., fadbann, ib. N.
ad-coillim *I destroy, ruin* 245.
ái *a cause*, n. pl. ái 153, 174.
áibne f. *delightfulness* 23.
aigne m. *a pleader, counsel*, dag-a. 178.
ailbéimm n. *a reproach* 30.
áilde f. *beauty* 206.
aill .. aill *once ... again, now ... now* 235.
ainchess *bodily pain*, acc. cen ainchiss 119. (ainces N).
ainmne f. *patience* 192, 251, dat. ainmnit 143. (ainmnet N).
ainmnetach *patient* 174, 189.
airberntas (airnbertas) m. (?) 180, 181.
airbert *a using, employing* 178.
air-gorad *a scorching* 140.
airisiu *a narration, tale*, cétna airisiu, Cóir Amn. 80. n. pl. airisena 102,125.
airmed *a certain dry measure* 138. Corm. Tr. 68.. eirmed, .i. tomus, 4, 3, 18, 70ª. dorat do Patraic in n-airmid mini, Trip. 186, 9.
aithech-borg m., aithech-port m. *a rent-paying town* 33.
aithne n. (later f.) *a deposit* 87, 157, 249.; aithne ṡalainn 87 L.
alaig *behaviour, demeanour* 86.
all n. *a rock*, n. pl. trí all 200.
allabair *an echo* 107.; O'Dav. 144.
ana *wealth* 147, 239.
áne f. *agility, deftness, skill* 84.
an-ergnaid *undignified* 221.
an-faitches m. *carelessness* 162.
an-fiad *a bad welcome* 70.
an-gar *unfilial, impious* 159, 235.
an-idna f. *impurity* 109.
an-richt m. *a misshapen person* 84.
antrenn *rough ground*, gen. antreinn 147.
apaig *ripe* 68.
ar-cuillim *I destroy, ruin* 184.; verb-noun, gen. aircaillti, ib. (N).
ard-nemed m. *a high dignitary* 157.
árech (árach) (1) *a tie, fetter*, gen. cú áraig 168.; (2) *a bond, surety*, acc. pl. cen áirche 74.; cin gealladh, cin airge, Laws II. 78, 4.
argius *instruction* (?), a. aiste 256. Cf. felmac fri ré na argaisi, Laws V. 364, 17.
aroslicim *I open*, aroslicet 204.
árus *residence, habitation* 218, 239.
ata *which are* 68, 69, 75, 76, &c.
ataid (?) 181.

ath-chommus m. *renunciation of control or authority* 160.

athchosan, better athchomsan (later achmusan) *a complaining* 98.; tossach augrai athchosan, LL. 345b18.

augra *strife* 213.

aupthach *veneficus* 185.

aurla (1) *a long lock of hair*, .i. ciab, Corm. Tr. 166; (2) *a person wearing* aurla, *a serf* (?); mac aurlai (erlai) 152.

báithe *foolishness* 252.

banas m. *womanhood*, gen. dag-banais 180.; droch-banais 181.

ban-chorr f. *a she-heron* 237.

ban-lá *a lucky day for women* 216.

belach n. *a mountain-pass*, n. pl. belaige 50.[Pg 48]

beó-athair m. *a live father* 151. Compare the following extract from H. 3, 18, p. 19*b*: *Cest.* Cid diatá "ní nais ná torbais"? Ar atáit nadmanna naisce ni na torbongat, ar ni rochat a nadmann naisce .i. mac beoathar for a athair, céile for a flaith, manach for a airchindech, hulach for inn ail*e*, ar ní tobongat díb ar comrac, acht atá folaith gaibthi friu.

béss *perhaps* 136.

binnech *melodious*, bó b. 85.

birit, f. *a sow*, gen. birite, 148. BM.

bithbenach m. *a criminal* 92. B.

bocc m. *a buck*, *he-goat*, n. pl. buicc 230.

boccacht f. *buckishness*, *obstinacy* 101, 102.

bolcra (?) 231. Cf. bolcaire m. *a hector*, O'Gr. Cat. 584, 4.

bolc-srónach *having distended nostrils* 231.

bothach m. *a hut-dweller*, *cottar* 150.

brén-ḟinn *stinking or rotten hair*, acc. pl. -a 105.

brodna (?) gen. brodnai 230.

bronn-galar m. *a disease of the abdomen* 224.

brugaide f. *keeping a hostel*, *hospitality* 134.

búadnas *a triumph*, *excellence*, n. pl. -a 88. H.

cáer comraic 121. note.

cáin-thocad m. *fair fortune*, dat. cáin-thocud 110.

calad *hard* 176.; fer c. 147.

cetludche f. *lustfulness* 209.

círmaire m. *a comb-maker* 117.

cisne *what are?* 239.

clithcha f. *comfort* (of dress) 182.

clochrad (clochrach?) *a stone building*(?) (from clochur?), n. pl. trí clochraid 34.

clúanaige m. *a rogue* 90, 104.

co-cless *performing feats together* 125.

cóemna *comfort*, *good cheer* 6, 46.

coim (coimm) *a cloak* 130.

coimgne (com-ecne) *synchronistic knowledge*; fer coimgni 248. = fer cumocni, Rev. Celt. vi. 165, 11.

coire *a caldron* 220. c. érma, c. goriath, c. áiged 127.

com-ar (W. cyf-ar) *holding ploughland in common* 125.

com-chissiu *an examination* 119.

com-líth *equally lucky* 217.

comneibe (?) 169.

com-rith (fri) *a racing together* 117.
con-beraim *I bear liabilities* 168.
condailbe f. *attachment*, *bias* 193, 252.
congna (collective) *horns* 105, 117.
con-rannaim *I share* 164.
con-tibim *I mock* 82.
córad-gein *a champion birth* 148. BM.
crann-dretel (?) 231.
crésine f. *piety* 196.
crossán m. *a buffoon* 116.
cúacróessach (?) 231.
cuilmen *a volume*, *tome* 62.
cuinnmíne f. *kindliness* 208.
daintech *biting* 168.; gl. dentatus Sg. 159.^{b}2.
debuid f. *strife* 98.
déicsiu *a seeing*, *spying*, gen. déicsen 43.
deinmne *impatience*, dat. deinmnait 144.
deirmitiu *irreverence*, gen. deirmiten 214.
derc *a hole*, *cave* 42.; dat. i nderc a oxaille, LU. 70^{a}45; resiu dorattar isin deirc, Lism. fo. 43^{b}1.
déss f. *land*, acc. déiss 167. (dés N); acc. pl. déissi, ib. L. See Cáin Adamnáin, p. 46.
dí-ainme f. *an unblemished state* 119.
dían-apud *a sudden notice* 235.
dí-araig *a person without bonds* (árach) 235.
díbe *a refusing*, *denying* 212, LL 117^{a}43, 121^{b}9, 188^{a}2, 188^{b}33.
díbech *refusing*, *denying* 95.; .i. diultadach, C. 1, 2.
dí-chuimne f. *lack of memory* 245.; ar dermat nó díchumni, [Pg 49]LL. 74^{a}30.
dí-galrae f. *sicklessness* 119.
dí-grad n. *hatred* 217.
dímainche f. *uselessness* 81.
dímainecht f. *uselessness* 81. H.
dímosc (?) 172.
dínnime f. *meanness*, *lowliness* 191.; ferr trumma dínnimi, LL. 345^{c}30. Cf. dín[n]imus, Alex. 996.
dirna *a stone* 237.
dí-sceóil *taleless* 248.
díthechte f. *non-possession* 219.
díthir *a landless person*, gen. díthir (díthire N) 165.
díthrub m. *a desert*, *uninhabited place*, n. pl. díthruib 43. In the later language it is inflected like *treb* (n.p. díthreba 43 BM).
diúite f. *simplicity* 24; LL. 294^{a}38. d. cridi, Lism. Lives 4543: Diúide ingen Slánchridi, Rawl. B. 512, 112^{2}b2.
diultadach (diultach) *fond of refusing* 96 MB.
dlúithe f. *compactness*, *obscurity* (?) (of speech) 179.
doas m. *ignorance* 245.
do-celaim *I hide* 84, 85.
dochell *niggardliness* 144; Dochall ⁊ Díbe ⁊ Do[th]chernas, Rawl. B. 512, 112^{b}1.
dochlatu m. *ill repute*. gen. dochlatad 212.
do-chond m. *an imbecile*, gen. dochuind 153.

dochraite f. *oppression* 153. Alex. 367, atchota daidbre d., LL. 345c3.

dodeime (?) 237 (todeime L).

dochta f. *closeness* 203.

do-delb *a misshapen person*, acc. la dodelb (dodeilb B) 84.

dofortaim *I pour out, spill, spoil, ruin*, dofortat 186; dofortatar .i. dotodsat, Ml. 124d12.

do-gnás f. *ill-breeding* 81; gen. dognáise 209.

doingthe f. *foulmouthedness* 252; for do-thengthe.

doingthes m. *id.* 213.

dolud *loss, damage* 198; gen. mét tar ndolaid, LL. 172b33; in cach níth ba dáel dolaid, 157b14.

dommatu m. *poverty* 198, Alex. 847.

dorenaim *I pay a fine* (díre) 158.

dotcad m. *misfortune*, n. pl. dotcaid 44, 64, 65, 71.

dotcadach *unfortunate* 135.

doth *a hatching*, cach d. toirthech, LL. 293b48; gen. in doithe 237; dat. do duth, ib.; gen. pl. cerce trí ndoth, O'Dav. 1375.

do-tongim *I swear*, ná dítoing 159.

drithlennach *full of sparks* 65.

drús f. *folly*; gen. drúise 193.

duine-chin m. *human crime* 168.

dul in the phrases, dul ar *to go security on behalf of* 235; dul fri *to go security for* 235. See Glossary to Laws s.v. dul.

dulbaire f. *lack of eloquence, bad delivery* 179.

dulsaine f. *mockery* 142; in cerd mac húi Dulsine, Corm. 37. Cf. dulaige, O'Dav. 622.

dúthracht f. *good will, kindliness* 225.

ech usci *a water-horse* 236.

echmuir(?) 184.

eisíne *a young bird* 237.

eó m. *a salmon*: gen. iach 92; n. pl., iaich, LL. 297a34.

eochair *a key* n. pl. eochracha 204.

erchoille (?) 230.

erdonal f. *a trumpeter, piper*; eardanal .i. stucaire no píobaire, BB. 65 m.s. acc. cen erdonail 253.

érim n. *a course, running*, gen. érma 127. Later fem., ar tressa na hérma, LL. 110a13.

erlam *ready* 239.

errad n. *dress, attire*: gen. erraid 233.

escaine *a curse* 20.

esconn *excommunicated* 235.

escra *a cup for drawing wine* 231.

éscus (é-scíss) m. *unweariedness* 110 (esces N). daurnaisce .i. aurlattu nó greschae nó escas, H. 3, 18, 80a.[Pg 50]

eserni (?) 231.

eserte f. *landlessness, vagrancy* 74.

espatu m. *frivolity* 214.

étach (verb-n. of in-tugur, O'Mulc. 462) n. *a dress*; gen. étaig 182.

étaid *jealous* 95.

etargaire *a separating, interposing, mediating*, 135, 154; LL. 31b15; dligid ugra e. 345d10.

etir-chert *a decision* 175.

faigdech (foigdech.) m. *a beggar* 83, Aisl. M. 71, 21.

faiscsiu *closeness* (?) 192 (faicsi N).

fássach *a precedent* 178; brithemnacht ar roscadaib ⁊ fasaigib, LU. 118[b].

fáthaige f. *the gift of prophecy* 192.

fáth-rann m. *a witty quatrain* 89; do fáthrannaib espa ⁊ airchetail, Otia Mers. III., p. 47, § 2.

fechemnas m. *debtorship* 170.

féige f. *sharpness, sagacity* 78.

feras m. *manhood, man's estate,* gen. dag-ferais 196; droch-ferais 197. Cf. feras léiginn *lectorship* AU.

fer-lá n. *a lucky day for men* 217.

fescred (feiscre N.) 118 = feascradh '*shrivelling, decaying,*' O'R. Cf. feasgor .i. dealugud, Lec. Voc. 403: dligid cach forcradach féscred, LL. 294[a]9.

fiad *a welcome.* n. pl. fiada (fiad L) 70.

fidchell (?) 142.

fid-nemed n. *a sacred grove, sanctuary*;[TN 158] '*lucus,*' BB. 469[a]46, O'Mulc. 830, n. pl. fidnemeda fírdorchra ⁊ cráeb-chaill comdígainn, C. Cath.

flett see plett.

fliuchaim *I wet*, rotfliuchus, 104.

fodb m. *accoutrement*, n. pl. fuidb 135.

fo-crenaim (verb-n. fochraic) *I bribe* 261.[TN Yes, printed as 261]

foglaid m. *a robber*, gen. foglada 92.

fo-glúaisim *I move* (trans.) 198.

foichell f. *hire, wages*, gen. foichle 13.

foichne *a blade of green corn* 75: ith-ḟoichne .i. foichne in etha, O'Dav. 1080.

1. foilmnech *roped, leashed*, cú f. 169.

2. foilmnech (fo-lémnech) *ready to leap* 91, 238.

foimrimm *a using, usucaption*, gen. foille foimrimme, LL. 344[c]55; n. pl. -e 163, Laws.

fóindledach m. *a waif* 198.

foll-derb f. *a milk-pail*, dat. hi foll-deirb 75, Laws.

fóindel m. *a straying*, n. pl. fóindil 181.

fomailt (verb-n. of fo-melim) f. *usufruct* 87.

fomus (verb-n. of fo-midiur) m. *calculation* (?) 118; béim co fomus, LU. 73[a]1. béim co fommus, LL. 74[a]26. roláosa, ol sé, fomus forsaní sin, LU. 58 24.

fo-naidm n. *a contract* 202.

for-íadaim *I close upon* 203.

for-ind-fedaim *I relate.* forindet 191: O'Dav. 511.

forngaire *a proclaiming* 140.

forrach *a measuring-rod* 138, O'Don. Suppl.

for-ṡnaidm (= for-naidm, with epenthetic *s*) n. *an overreaching* (?) 186: co fornadmaim níad náir, LU. 73[a]7.

fortgellaim *I give evidence, bear witness* 138.

for-tongim *I swear*, fortoinger (fortongar) 158.

fossad *steady, firm* 174 (fossaid N).

fossugud *stability* 28.

fosta f. *staidness, steadiness* 180, 187, 194, 215, 218.

fotha n. *foundation*, f. n-utmall 173. Cf. ní cóir in fotha utmall, Sg. 4[b].

fothirbe *a field* (?) 56, Trip. 82, 2; 168, 26.

freccor (verb-n. of fris-curim) *opposition, objection* 154, ML 131[a]8.

frecra (verb-n. of fris-garim) n. *an answer* 174.

frith-nóill *a counter-oath* 165.

fúaimm n. *a din, noise* 146, f. nglan, LL. $150^{b}4$; f. in churaig risin tracht, YBL 89^{b}; n. pl. fúammann 146.

fúatche f. *a snatching, carrying off* 140.[Pg 51]

fuchacht (fuichecht) f. *copulation, cohabitation* 155.

fuigliur *I pronounce judgment*, fuigletar 161.

fuirec (verb-n. of foricim) m. *preparation*, n. pl. fuiric 97, 98.

fuirmed *a sitting, placing*, gen. aithne fuirmeda, 157.

fuirsire m. *a juggler* 241.

gáir *a cry, shout*, n. pl. gártha 99 M.

gáis f. *wisdom* 177, gen. gáisse 178, 192, 251.

gáisse f. *wisdom*, acc. cen gáissi 176.

gait (verb-noun of gataim) f. *a taking away, carrying off*, gen. fer gaite meirle 141.

gamnach f. *a stripper*, gen. gamnaige 234.

gart *generosity* 240.

gatach *thievish* 185.

geir (?) 231.

gen f. *a smile* 91, n. pl. gena, *ib.*

genmnaide *chaste* 187, genmnaide ben aenfir, H. 3, 18, 79^{b}.

glass m. *a lock*, n. pl. glais 203.

goirt *salted*, bíad g. 70.

goriath (?) 127.

grainne (?) 231.

gréss *handicraft* 70, ferr g. soos, LL. $345^{c}51$.

gríss *heat, fever, ardour, fervour* 224; colum co crábud, co ngrís, LL. $35^{a}48$.

grith *a cry, shout* 99, n. pl. gretha, *ib.*

grúss (?) 143.

gúala *a large vessel, vat* 255; n. pl. gúala, *ib.* Cf. iern-gúala.

íach (a late nom. formed from the oblique cases of eó) m. *a salmon*, gen. iaich 92, L.

íarduibe f. *after-grief* 67. Cf. íarnduba.

íarmur f. *remnant, leavings* 65.

íarnduba f. *after-grief* 125, 141.

íarraid *foster-fee* 149.

im-bánad *a growing pale* 188.

im-gellad *a pledging oneself* 101.

immarchor *a conveying about or across* 239.

immed n. *plenty* 178, 225.

imreson, O. Ir. imbressan (verb-n. of im-fresnaim) f. *a wrangling* 101,252, acc. pro nom. imresain 193.

imraichne *a mistake* 101, imraithne 229 N.

im-thomailt f. *food* 149.

im-crenaim *pay or buy mutually*, imuscrenat 170.

ind-chosc m. *an indication*, n. pl. ind-choisc 254.

in-crenaim *I pay, buy* 155. Enclitic: ní écriae. Ériu 1., p. 199, §21.

ír f. *wrath* 188. O'Dav. 1103.

itfa (?) 231. Cf. itfaide toile, LL. $344^{c}36$.

labor *talkative* 248; bat l. fri labra, bat tó fri tó, LL. $346^{a}12$.

lán *the full-tide* 237.

laxa f. *inertness* 212.

lén *sloth* 243; tossach lubra lén, LL. 345b33.

lethiu *broader*, *wider* 235.

lia m. *a stone*, dat. liic 147.

litánacht f. *singing the litany*, 14.

lobra = lomrad *a stripping* 218; gen. lomartha, *ib.*

luaithrind *a pair of compasses*, gen. lúd -e 118; fo chosmailius luaithrinde, Corm. 13, s.v. Coire Brecáin.

luchra *a smile* 238.

lúd = lúth *agility*, *quick motion* 118. Wi. nimtha lúd hi cois nó il-láim, LU. 16a5.

mad *well*, ní mad bíadsam, ní mad ríadsam 236.

máil *blunt*; *simple-minded*, *witless*, ingen m. 114.

méile f. *lewdness* 228; ben méile 223.[Pg 52]

marb-dil *dead chattel*, Laws. acc. pl. marbdili 105.

med *a balance*, *scales* 138.

meirle f. *theft* 141.

mer-aichne *a mistake* 229.

meraige m. *a fool*, *fop* 103.

mí-airle *evil counsel* 243; tossach míarli malartcha, LL. 345b37.

midlachas m. *cowardice* 197.

mí-gairm n. *an evil cry*, nom. du. dá m. 124.

miscne, miscena (n. pl.) *hatreds* 179, 248.

mí-thocad m. *misfortune*, *ill-luck*, gen. míthocaid 124; dat. míthocod109.

mblecht (mblicht) *in milk* 146.

móaigim *I increase*, verb-n. gen. móaigthe 146.

muilleóir m. *a miller*, gen. muilleórach 234.

muimme f. *a nurse*, n. pl. muime 246, 247, muimmecha 130.

muin *neck*, *back*, in the phrase do m. 232 = de mhuin *because of*, *in consequence of*, Dinneen.

nemed, m. *a privileged person*, gen. nemid filed 255.

nem-idna f. *impurity* 109 BM.

nemthigur *I constitute*, neimthigedar 116-123, 202: Corm. s.v. níth: rofogluim sium in tréide nemthigius filid, Megn. Finn 19.

neóit *churlishness*, *niggardliness* 144.

ness (1) .i. aurnise criad *a clay furnace*, H. 3, 18, 73b; gen. fri derc a neis, Corm. 33, 2; (2) *the wooden mould or block in which the furnace of moist, soft clay, was formed*;[128] bói crann ina láim .i. neas a ainm ⁊ is uime dogníther an urnise criad, Corm. 32 s. v. nescoit; (3) .i. mála cré *a bag of (moulding) clay* H. 1, 15.

[128]I owe this explanation to Dr. P.W. Joyce.

nóill *an oath* 165 (náill N); n. pl. nóill, ib.

ochán *an urging*, *egging on* 112. Cf. achain, Boroma 122.

ochtrach (later otrach) f. *a dunghill*, ML 129c2; dat. for ochtraig 117(otrach N).

óc-thigern m. *a franklin* 71.

óil f. *a cheek*, gen. óile 116.

oirce *a lap-dog* 241.

ordan *dignity*, gen. ordain 246, 254. With Triad 246, compare the following extract from H. 3, 18, p. 9*b*: Secht rann fichet (xx .i. MS) triasa (friasa MS) toet feab ⁊ ordan (ordain MS) do duine: tria gaireui, tria ainmnit, tria ḟostai, tria thói, tria f*or*sadi, tria fogluim, tri domestai, tri étsecht fírindi, tri chocad fri clóine, tri indarb*a* anfis, tri thochur[i]ud fis, tri trebairei, tri coitsecht fri forrsaidi, tri frecmorc fíren, tri filidhecht téchtai, tri ailge auscuichthi, tri airmitin sen, tri denam sinsire, tri ermitin flatha, tri airmidin ecnai, tri honoi[r] fithidre, tri timorgain cuibsi *nó*gnúisi, tri idhnai lámai, tri congain cuibsi, tri imrád bá[i]s, tria imrád *nó*décsin i nDia na ndúla.

paitt f. *a leather bottle*, p. meda, LL. 117^{a}50; LU. 54^{b}22; gen. paitte231; na paitte, LL. 117^{b}2; du. n. dá phait f̃ina, LB. 129^{a}.

plett (flett) f. *an edge* 121; plet .i. nomen rinda dogníat cerda, H. 3, 18, p. 73: flét, O'R.

prap-chaillte (literally 'sudden hardness') f. *closefistedness* 212.

ráth f. *security*, *surety* 235; gen. rátha 139.

ráthaiges m. *guarantorship* 135, 248.

rathmaire f. *bountifulness* 211.

reclés *an abbey-church* 11.

reithe m. *a ram* 117, 168.[Pg 53]

rige *a stretching*, *extending* 116.

rigne (raigne) f. *stiffness* 179: LL. 212^{b}15; rigne labartha, 345^{d}10.

roimse *abundance* 202.

ronn *a chain* 121.

rop m. *a brute*, n. pl. ruip, 168, 169. With Triad 168 compare the following extract from H. 3, 18, p. 8^{b}: Rofesar rupu tria fóindel caich laithiu dosliat fiachui dóine do cethrai .i. each cen cuibrich cech tráthai, cú cen cuibrech *nó* cen lomain laithe, muiccai cen mucalaig ndorcha.

ros-chullach m. *a stallion* 114.

ro-thé very hot, *scalding* 70; Aisl. M.

rucca f. *shame* 143.

ruire m. *a king*, gen. pl. ruirech 202.

rúss *a blushing* 143; O'Dav. 1336, 1343, rús .i. grúaid, ut dicitur: co nach romna rús richt. Rús dono imdergad ⁊ gach nderg, H. 3, 18, 73^{c}.

sail *a beam*, *prop*, n. pl. sailge 101.

saill f. *fat*, *bacon* 170; gen. cia tiget na saille, LB. 260^{b}20; n pl. sailltí184.

sain-chor m. *a special contract*, gen. -chuir 151.

salánach *dirty*, *filthy*, n. pl. salanaig 230.

saltraim *I trample*, rosaltrus 104.

sámtha *repose* 189.

sant f. *avarice* 115.

scenb *a startling* (?) n. pl. scenb 106.

scéo *and* 223.

scolóc *a young student* 233.

secnabbóite f. *vice-abbotship* 46.

seche *a hide*, *skin* 230.

ségainn *accomplished*; *an accomplished person*, n. pl. ségainni, 89(ségaind M ségainn N); ní rabha i nEirinn uile budh griabhdha nó bud segaine inás, Three Fragm. 34.

seim *a rivet* 172.

seol (seola) *child-bed* 224.

sírecht f. *a tabu*, .i. geis, O'Dav. 1482, who quotes triad 253.

sirite m. *a wild man*, *sprite* 114.

sit *hush*! 137; sit sit! Hib. Min. 78, 23.

sleith f. *cohabiting with a woman without her knowledge* 155; Aisl. M. O'Dav. 97.

slissén *a chip*, *lath* 169.

snáth f. *a thread*, gen. snáithe 75.

so-bés m. *good manners* 84.

sobraid *sober* 251; sobraig, LL. 343d3; sobraig cách co haltram, LL. 345d45.

sobraide f. *sobriety* 187, 251.

sochell *liberality* 210; LL. 345b39.

sochlatu m. *good repute*, gen. sochlatad 211.

sochoisc *docile* 251; n. pl. -e, CZ. III. 451, 28.

sochoisce f. *docility* 194; tossach suthi s., LL. 345b23.

so-delb f. *a fine figure* 85.

so-gnás f. *good breeding* 210; gen. sognáise 208.

soithnges m. *wellspokenness* 208, 251.

soitcedach *fortunate* 239.

somnath (ˣso-múnad) *easily taught, docile* 251. Cf. O'Dav. 1481.

somnathe f. *docility* 251.

són *that* 239.

sotcad m. *good fortune*, gen. sotcaid 210.

sotla f. *pride* 247.

so-thengtha *well-spoken* 251.

sproicept *a preaching* 111 B. sproicepht M.

sreb f. 'the stream of milk drawn from a cow's teats at each tug,' Dinneen; gen. sreibe, 75 L.

sreb immais 112 note.

srithid f. '*the passage of milk from the breast*.' O'R.: gen. srithide 75.

sruithe f. *seniority* 5.

sta *hush!* 137; Bodl. Corm. stata, Hib. Min. 78, 1.

súarcus m. *mirth* 210.

suirge f. *a courting, wooing*, 247.

suthaine f. *lastingness*, 182.[Pg 54]

tacra *a pleading*, t. fergach 173 = LL. 345d23.

tairisiu m. *trustfulness* 204.

tairismige f. *obduracy* 209.

tair-leimm n. *an alighting, a place of alighting*; geis dí tochim cen tairlim, LL. 201a11: n. pl. tairleme, 32.

taisec *restitution, restoration* 157. Laws, Aisl. M.

tal-chaire f. *self-will, obstinacy* 131.

tarcud *a proposing* 72, 73; t. do drochmnái, Aisl. M. 73, 26.

tarsunn m. *a sauce*; tarsand, O'Mulc. 612: n. pl. tarsuinn 184 (tarsunn L): torsnu, Aisl. M. 99, 7.

tascor *a retinue*, t. ríg 71, t. ríg nó espuic, O'Dav. 1501.

1. téite f. *wantonness* 18.

2. téite *a fair, gathering* 88.

tenn (teinn, tinn) *sore, hurting*, cluiche t. 90. Cf. mían leisan laoch lúaiter linn | cluiche ó nách biad duine tinn *a game by which no one is hurt*, Bruss. MS. 2569, fo. 65a.

tirdacht f. *boorishness* 229.

tlás f. *weariness* 132, 133.

togním. m. (?) 219.

toicthiu (?) 131.

toimtiu f. *opinion* 136. Cf. mac toimten '*son of conjecture*,' O'Dav. 1596.

tothucht *substance* 85. BB. 19b14.

tradna *a corncrake* 129.

trecheng *a triad*. For O.-Ir. trethenc, Wb. 29c5 (Thes. I. 691).

trichem *a fit of coughing*; sen-t. 114. mod. tritheamh.

trichtach *example, pattern* (?) 27. is é did*iu* in fer sin ropo trichtach do Chorinntib ara techtatis an indmus am*al* ná techtatis, LB. 146ª32; ropo trichtach tra don eclais dílgedaig fo chosmailius ingen n-óg ná tabrat olc ar olc, acbt logud, *ib*.

tromdatu m. *importunity* 214.

tromm m. *the elder-tree* 129; gen. connud truimm, RC. VII., 298, 3.

trú *a doomed person*, dat. robud do throich 83 = Aisl. M. 71, 20.

trumma f. *weightiness, self-importance* 131.

trusca f. *leprosy* 133 N.; clam-trusca AU. 950.

tuilféth *a frown* 142.

tuisledach *stumbling, offending* 96 N.

turtugud *a compelling, forcing, violating* 155: is tar turtugud nDé ⁊ Patraic cach gell ⁊ cach aitire, Cáin Domn.; LU. 74ª19, 123ª17; turtugud breth, LL. 344ᵇ; turrtugad .i. timpud, H. 3, 18, 539ᵇ; a turtad .i. per uim, O'Dav. 1151; turtad .i. coméicniugud, O'Mulc. H. 3, 18, 74ᵇ, 866.

uais *hard, difficult* 220, 235; coruice uais nó angbocht, .i. is é iu t-uais ní ná raibe aice féin, O'Dav. 112.